The scene above Longarm was imprinted on his brain in an instant. Jimmy Lloyd stood to his left, holding the Winchester loosely as he gaped down open-mouthed at Longarm. Mitch Rainey was to the right, the shovel he had been using to throw dirt on Longarm still gripped in both of his hands. The derringer gave a spiteful little crack as it sent a bullet through the open mouth of Lloyd. The outlaw was thrown backward as the slug bored up through his brain and burst out the back of his skull.

"Damn!" Mitch Rainey yelled as he flung the shovel aside wildly and grabbed for the pistol holstered on his hip. However, Longarm had tracked the derringer to the right by the time Rainey's fingers slapped the butt of his Colt. The little weapon spat its second lead pellet.

Longarm aimed at Rainey's balls.

That seemed to be a good target from his angle . . .

TABOR EVANS

LONGARM

AND THE BRAZOS DEVIL

JOVE BOOKS, NEW YORK

LONGARM AND THE BRAZOS DEVIL

A Jove Book / published by arrangement with
the author

PRINTING HISTORY
Jove edition / March 1996

The Putnam Berkley World Wide Web site address is
http://www.berkley.com

ISBN: 0-515-11828-1

A JOVE BOOK®
Jove Books are published by The Berkley Publishing Group,
200 Madison Avenue, New York, New York 10016.
JOVE and the "J" design are trademarks
belonging to Jove Publications, Inc.

PRINTED IN THE UNITED STATES OF AMERICA

10 9 8 7 6 5 4 3 2 1

Chapter 1

Clods of dirt hitting him in the back of the head woke Long-arm up.

He tasted dirt in his mouth too, and it took an effort on his part not to gag and spit it out. He didn't want Lloyd and Rainey to know he was conscious again, not until he was sure what was going on, anyway. Longarm already had a pretty good idea.

He figured he was lying facedown in the grave the two polecats had made him dig, and that dirt pattering down around him meant they were filling up the hole.

They were burying him alive.

Longarm repressed a shudder at the thought. His theory was confirmed a moment later when a harsh but familiar voice said from somewhere above him, ''Hell, Mitch, I thought sure he'd wake up by now. How hard did you hit him with that shovel anyway?''

''Not hard enough to kill him,'' Mitch Rainey replied. Another shovelful of dirt thudded down on Longarm's back this time.

''It'd be a lot more fun if he knew we were puttin' him in the ground like this. Reckon if he wakes up in time he'll start screamin' and beggin' for his life?''

"I doubt it, Jimmy. He said his name was Long, so I figure he's the one they call Longarm. He's got quite a rep.''

Longarm heard a spitting sound. Jimmy Lloyd said, ''Shoot, he didn't look so high-an'-mighty to me, not the way we got the drop on him and made the poor bastard dig his own grave 'fore you clouted him.''

More dirt hit Longarm in the back of the head.

"We were lucky,'' Mitch said. "If he hadn't been so sick, we wouldn't have been able to sneak up on him like that.''

That was damn sure true, Longarm thought bitterly. If he hadn't eaten that bad beef last night over at Pickettville, none of this would have happened. If he hadn't been on his hands and knees puking his guts out, a couple of two-bit owlhoots like Rainey and Lloyd would never have gotten within a hundred yards of him without him being aware of it. Longarm didn't know what tasted worse in his mouth: Texas dirt, leftover vomit—or failure.

But he wasn't dead yet, he reminded himself . . . just half-buried.

The dirt was piling up around his head and shoulders and torso, filling the narrow gaps between his body and the sides of the rough grave. Longarm lifted his head a fraction of an inch, not enough to be noticed by the two killers standing above him. That allowed him to breathe a little easier, although the air was still dense with the smell of damp earth. He had fallen with his right arm underneath him when Rainey belted him from behind with a shovel, which was as close to a lucky break as he was likely to get. He could move his hand a little without Rainey and Lloyd seeing what he was doing.

Trouble was, that hand and arm were more than half numb from the weight of his body lying on them. He couldn't be certain his muscles were going to do what he wanted when he called on them for action. He flexed his fingers against his belly, trying to work some feeling back into them.

He had heard the two outlaws coming earlier, but not in time to do much more than straighten up from his undignified

2

position. Lloyd had rammed the muzzle of a Winchester into his back and Rainey had grabbed his arm, then reached over and plucked Longarm's .44 from its cross-draw rig. Hauled unceremoniously to his feet, Longarm had had no choice but to go along with the two outlaws for the moment, in hopes of finding an opportunity to turn the tables on them.

The opportunity hadn't come. Rainey and Lloyd might not be any great shakes as outlaws, but they were careful. They had both stood well back and covered him with their rifles while they forced him to dig a hole with one of their shovels. They had laughed and hooted at him while they discussed what they were going to do to the no-good lawdog they had captured. Longarm had seethed, but that had been all he could do. Then, while Lloyd kept jabbering, Rainey had come up behind Longarm with the extra shovel and whacked him a good one on the back of the head. He was lucky the blow hadn't caved in his skull, Longarm knew. But as Rainey had just admitted, he hadn't intended to kill the deputy United States marshal. He and his companion wanted Longarm alive so that they could savor his death.

They had made a mistake, though. They had gotten his handgun, but they didn't know about the little two-shot derringer attached to his watch chain and hidden inside his vest.

The derringer around which Longarm's fingers had just closed.

Cautiously, he worked the weapon free from the pocket of his vest and tightened his grip on it. Pins and needles shot up and down his arm, but at least he could feel something again in that extremity. He would have a chance—maybe not a fair shake, but at least a chance—and that was all he had ever asked for in life since he had left West-by-God Virginia all those years ago.

"Don't cover up his head all the way," Lloyd said with a cackle of laughter. "I still want him to wake up. Put some dirt on his feet instead."

No point in postponing things any longer, Longarm decided. He was as ready as he was going to be. He flipped over as fast as he could in the narrow grave and said, "I'm alive, Jimmy." His fist came up out of the loose dirt with the derringer clutched in it. He hoped like blazes that all the grit hadn't fouled the firing mechanism.

The scene above him was imprinted on his brain in an instant. Jimmy Lloyd stood to his left, holding the Winchester loosely as he gaped down open-mouthed at Longarm. Mitch Rainey was to the right, the shovel he had been using to throw dirt on Longarm still gripped in both of his hands. The derringer gave a spiteful little crack as it sent a bullet through the open mouth of Lloyd. The outlaw was thrown backward as the slug bored up through his brain and burst out the back of his skull.

"Shit!" Mitch Rainey yelled as he flung the shovel aside wildly and grabbed for the pistol holstered on his hip. However, Longarm had tracked the derringer to the right by the time Rainey's fingers slapped the butt of his Colt. The little weapon spat its second lead pellet.

Longarm was aiming at Rainey's balls. That seemed to be a good target from his angle, and the shot would have sure as hell put the outlaw on the ground if it had gone home. Instead, though, Rainey's contortions as he struggled to draw his gun turned his body just enough so that Longarm's bullet merely clipped him on the outside of the right hip. Rainey staggered back, yelling in pain.

Bending himself almost double with the effort, Longarm jackknifed up out of the grave. It was only about four feet deep because Rainey and Lloyd had gotten tired of standing there and watching Longarm dig. The lawman put his hands on the ground and pushed himself up, vaulting into the air as he emerged from the hole. He came out to the left, toward the spot where Lloyd had disappeared. The dead man was sprawled on the ground next to the grave, the fallen Winchester beside him.

Longarm dropped the empty derringer, flung out an arm, and grabbed the rifle's breech as he lowered his shoulder and rolled over the corpse. Rainey's gun blasted, but the bullet

4

thudded into Lloyd, who was long past being hurt by it. Longarm tumbled completely over and came up with his right hand through the lever of the Winchester. His finger found the rifle's trigger as he brought the barrel in line with Rainey on the other side of the long, narrow hole in the ground.

There had been no way for Longarm to know if the Winchester was ready to fire, but luck was with him again. The rifle bucked in his hands as it blasted. Rainey was scuttling away from the other side of the grave like a desperate crab. The outlaw went down hard, the impact as he landed on the ground knocking the gun out of his hand.

Longarm came up on one knee and levered the Winchester in the same motion, jacking another round into the rifle's chamber. He brought it to his shoulder, aiming at Rainey's fallen gun as the outlaw groped toward the Colt. Longarm fired. The bullet slammed into the revolver and kicked it a good dozen feet from Rainey's outstretched fingers. Longarm levered the rifle again and said, "The next one goes in your head, Mitch, unless you settle down and don't move again."

Rainey cussed a blue streak, but he remained motionless on the ground as Longarm climbed to his feet. He circled the grave, still covering Rainey with the Winchester. As far as Longarm could see, the outlaw had only had the one gun on him. Rainey's rifle was in the saddle boot of the Appaloosa tied to a bush about forty feet away, next to Lloyd's chestnut. The gray gelding Longarm had rented in a stable over in Weatherford a few days earlier seemed to have run off. Longarm didn't much care; the son of a bitch had had an uncomfortable gait about him. Billy Vail might pitch a fit, though, when the Justice Department got charged an inflated purchase price for the animal.

There was nothing Longarm could do about that now. He peered at Rainey over the barrel of the Winchester and asked, "Where'd I get you the second time, old son?" He couldn't see but one patch of blood on the outlaw's clothes, and that stain was on Rainey's hip.

"You only hit me the once, you bastard," Rainey said. He

pressed the palm of his hand against his hip and winced. "A rock rolled under my foot; otherwise I wouldn't have fallen down and you'd be a dead man now, Long!"

So luck had smiled on him yet again, Longarm thought. Well, it was only fair. If not for that tainted beef, he wouldn't have been in such a bad fix to start with, and the steak hadn't smelled or tasted bad. He made a mental vow to never again buy a meal in Pickettville, Texas, should he ever find himself there again.

"If you ain't injured, get up on your feet," he told Rainey.

"My hip's broke!" the outlaw protested.

Longarm sighed. "I doubt that mighty serious-like, the way you were squirming after that six-shooter you dropped a couple of minutes ago. That bullet just creased you, Rainey, but the next one sure as hell won't."

Muttering under his breath, Rainey climbed awkwardly to his feet. He listed to the right, favoring the injured hip, but he was able to stand up and hobble away from the grave.

Longarm checked Rainey's pistol. The cylinder had been smashed and the frame bent by the bullet from the Winchester; the gun was useless, not even worth picking up off the ground. Longarm went back around the grave to make sure Jimmy Lloyd was dead, not that there was much doubt in his mind. It was mighty difficult to survive having half your brain blown out the back of your head, and Lloyd hadn't managed to beat those odds.

Longarm found his own .44 stuck behind Lloyd's belt. He tugged the revolver loose and settled it back in the cross-draw rig, then took Lloyd's Colt as well. That done, he started trying to brush some of the dirt off his clothes. One good thing about the brown tweed which his trousers and coat were made from was that it didn't show mud stains too much.

"Hey!" Rainey yelled. "How long you going to make me stand here? I'm in pain, you know!"

"Ask me if I care," muttered Longarm. He spotted his flat-crowned, snuff-brown Stetson on the ground not far away and picked it up. It was none the worse for wear, since he had

6

already taken it off and set it aside earlier before he'd started throwing up.

He settled the hat on his head and brushed some dirt out of the wide, sweeping brown mustache on his upper lip. He spat a few times, clearing his mouth of the last of the grit and the aftertaste from being sick. A good healthy shot of Maryland rye would have cleaned his mouth even better, but what was left of the bottle he had bought in Weatherford had been carried off by that stupid gray horse. Longarm sighed again. The trials and tribulations of being a lawman sometimes made him wonder why he kept on packing a badge.

It wasn't like he wanted to go back to cowboying or scouting for the army, though. His years of riding for Uncle Sam's Justice Department had been eventful, dangerous ones, but he wouldn't have traded them for a more settled existence. Having to put up occasionally with murderous assholes like Rainey and Lloyd was the price he paid for the freedom he enjoyed.

"Stay where you are," Longarm advised Rainey. He went over to the Appaloosa and the chestnut. Rainey's Appaloosa was the better mount, which was not surprising considering that Rainey was the brains of the two-man outfit. According to the reports Longarm had read, Rainey had seemed to be in charge during the stagecoach holdups the two outlaws had carried out. He had probably planned the jobs, which had netted a few good payoffs and a lot of miserly ones. But the important thing as far as Longarm and his boss, Chief Marshal Billy Vail, were concerned was that several U.S. mail pouches had been stolen, making the crimes a federal matter.

Most of the time Vail would have contented himself with sending wires from the office in Denver to the Texas Rangers and the local law in these parts, advising them of the federal warrants that had been issued on Rainey and Lloyd. In this case, however, Billy had judged it prudent to find an excuse for getting Longarm out of town for a while, so he had sent his top deputy to Texas to run down the two outlaws. Longarm had sworn up and down that he hadn't known the pretty young redhead was actually the newlywed bride of an elderly but still

7

powerful Congressman, but to no avail.

He had taken the train to Fort Worth, caught a stagecoach to Weatherford, some twenty miles to the west, and rented a horse there. It hadn't taken him very long to get on the trail of Rainey and Lloyd, since they were proud of being desperadoes and took advantage of every opportunity to proclaim how bad they were to anybody who was willing to listen, but several days of riding in circles through this rugged Brazos River country had been required before he finally closed in on them.

And then his damned stomach had gone crazy on him, which was how he'd wound up facedown in a grave he had dug himself.

Now, surprisingly enough, his belly didn't feel too bad. He supposed he had gotten rid of everything that was upsetting it. In fact, he was a little hungry. After a night of feeling queasy, he hadn't eaten any breakfast this morning, so his insides were pretty empty.

Longarm untied the horses and led them over toward Rainey. "There's a town called Cottonwood Springs not far from here, if I recollect right," he said. "Ought to be a doctor there to look at your hip, and we can catch a stage there for Weatherford and Fort Worth."

"Where the hell you taking me?" demanded Rainey.

"Back to Denver, so you can be tried on those federal wants. You haven't killed anybody as far as I know, so I reckon you'll wind up in prison for a few years. You're a lot luckier than your partner, Rainey."

The outlaw didn't look like he considered himself lucky. He glowered at Longarm, and when the lawman told him to climb up on the chestnut, he said angrily, "That's Jimmy's horse. The Appaloosa's mine."

"I think you've got more to worry about than who rides which horse," Longarm told him in a deceptively mild voice. "Now climb up into that saddle."

Still complaining, Rainey did as he was told. Then he pointed at Lloyd's body and asked, "What about Jimmy? You can't just leave him laying out here for the buzzards and the wolves!"

"I suppose you're right," Longarm said. Keeping the Winchester pointed in Rainey's general direction, he walked over to the other outlaw and hooked the toe of his right boot underneath Lloyd's shoulder. "Since we've got a grave right handy . . ."

A powerful motion of Longarm's leg rolled the body into the hole. Lloyd's corpse thumped to the bottom of the grave.

"You want to cover him up?" Longarm asked.

Chapter 2

Calling Longarm a coldhearted son of a bitch and every other name he could think of, Rainey got down from the saddle and used one of the shovels to fill up the grave. Longarm could have sent the undertaker out from Cottonwood Springs to fetch in the body, but there seemed to be a certain irony in burying Lloyd here, the sort of thing the dime-novel writers called poetic justice. Besides, Billy Vail would accept Longarm's word for it that Jimmy Lloyd was buried good and proper, even if he didn't like it.

"I'm liable to bleed to death before you ever get me to town," Rainey said as he mounted up again.

"Doesn't look like that stain on your jeans is much bigger now than it was earlier," Longarm said. "Appears to me that wound's not much more than a bullet burn. You'll live to go to jail." Longarm paused, then added, "That's if you don't try anything else funny. If I have to kill you for resisting arrest, my boss won't ever question it. And I don't mind telling you, Rainey, I didn't want to come down here to Texas after a couple of two-bit badmen like you and your partner in the first place. My mood's just gotten worse since I've been here."

"You shouldn't ought to threaten a prisoner like that," Rainey whined.

"Just remember what I told you."

If the truth were known, Longarm thought, Billy Vail hated it when he sent his top deputy after prisoners and Longarm came back with either corpses or death certificates. But the men a deputy U.S. marshal usually tangled with weren't the sort you'd find singing hymns in a church choir on Sunday morning. A lawman out here on the frontier couldn't avoid shooting a few fellas every now and then. So Longarm hoped fervently that Mitch Rainey wouldn't give him any more trouble. But Rainey didn't have to know that.

It was early autumn, and the air here was crisp and clean, which only seemed to add to Longarm's hunger. The landscape was fairly rugged, with lots of hills and bluffs and little valleys. Cedar and post oak breaks dotted the terrain. From time to time, through gaps in the hills, Longarm caught a glimpse of a winding stream, and knew it was the Brazos River. He had crossed and recrossed the stream a dozen times in the past few days as he searched for his quarry. The summer had been a dry one, so the river was low in most places, a narrow, meandering flow that left much of the streambed dry and sandy. Further south, from around Waco on to the Gulf, the Brazos was a pretty good-sized river, but in this stretch and further west and north, in the Seven Fingers country, it didn't amount to much except in times of heavy rain. Then it could come roaring down through these gullies in a sudden flood.

Longarm's mind wasn't really on the river. He rode with one eye on his prisoner and the other eye on the trail. He hadn't given up all hope of running across that gray gelding. The jughead had taken off with all his possibles, including his own Winchester and the McClellan saddle that Longarm preferred to the stockman's model, which was what was cinched onto the Appaloosa's back. If he was able to recover his gear, it would improve his disposition a little.

In the meantime, he was still hungry, so he guided the Appalloosa with his knees and began rummaging in Rainey's saddlebags. "You got anything to eat in here?" he asked.

"You stay out of them bags!" Rainey yelped. "What's in there is none of your business, Long. Hell, you're nothing but a damned thief hiding behind a badge."

"Oh, hush up," Longarm snapped, irritated. "I've got a right to search a prisoner's belongings for evidence—what the hell!"

He lifted his hand out of the bag and stared at the strands of glittering jewelry that hung from his fingers. The necklace and the bracelet were both decorated with an abundance of gems and precious stones. Longarm let out a low whistle.

"You put them baubles back!" Rainey shouted. "They're not yours!"

"Where in Hades did you get any loot like this?" asked Longarm. "The way I understood it, you and Lloyd didn't get much from those stage holdups except cash and some bonds. Unless you pulled another job recently that wasn't in the report I read." Longarm shook his head. "Anyway, what woman in her right mind would take a stagecoach ride wearing anything like this?"

Rainey glared at him. "Jimmy and I found that jewelry. We didn't steal it, I swear! So it's not evidence and you don't have any right to keep it."

Longarm snorted in disgust and said, "You expect me to believe you just *found* jewelry like this out in the middle of nowhere?"

"It's true, I tell you. Jimmy could tell you himself—if you hadn't shot him."

"Yeah, and I'm sure I'd believe him too," Longarm drawled. "If there's any law in Cottonwood Springs, I intend to ask him about these. Maybe he'll know where they came from."

Rainey still looked angry, but he didn't say anything else. Longarm was grateful for that. He put the necklace and bracelet in one of the inside pockets of his coat and resumed his search of the saddlebags. As far as he was concerned, what

12

he turned up next was even better than a handful of fancy jewelry.

"Bacon and biscuits!" he exclaimed. "You been holding out on me, Mitch. Got a fryin' pan anywhere in this gear?"

"Over here in Jimmy's saddlebag," Rainey answered reluctantly.

"When we find a good place, we'll stop and fry us up a mess of this bacon for lunch. That sound all right to you?"

"Sure. Why the hell not?" Rainey's tone was bitter, but Longarm ignored it.

They had been following a game trail for the past few minutes, and it led inevitably toward the river. As they came within sight of the Brazos once again, Longarm saw that the trail ended at a small clearing on the riverbank. He couldn't have asked for a better place to make a noon camp.

The two men rode into the clearing, which was surrounded by a thick growth of post oaks and live oaks. Longarm swung down from the saddle, taking Jimmy Lloyd's Winchester with him. Rainey's rifle was still in the boot. "You can get down now," Longarm told the outlaw. "We'll be here for a while."

Rainey dismounted, wincing as he did so. "Reckon you ought to take a look at this wound you gave me?" he asked. "I don't want it to fester up on me."

Longarm suspected Rainey just wanted to get close enough so that he could make a grab for a gun. With a shake of his head, Longarm said, "You'll be all right."

Rainey blew out his breath in a noisy sigh and started muttering about high-handed lawmen who killed a fella's partner and then didn't give a damn about whether or not a gent got blood poisoning from the bullet wound that the damned high-handed lawman had been responsible for in the first place. Longarm paid no attention to the complaints. Instead he gestured with the barrel of the Winchester in his hands and said, "Go over there to that post oak tree."

"What for?" Rainey asked with a suspicious frown.

"Just do it."

The outlaw walked slowly to the tree Longarm had indi-

13

cated, then said, "All right, I'm here. Now what?"

"Hug it."

Rainey's frown deepened as he pulled his head back to stare at Longarm. "What?"

"I said hug the tree."

"I'm an outlaw, damn it!" Rainey burst out. "I don't go around huggin' trees!"

"You do now," Longarm said calmly. He lifted the barrel of the rifle a little for emphasis.

Rainey rolled his eyes, gritted his teeth, then faced the tree and threw his arms around it. The trunk of the post oak was slender enough so that his arms easily encircled it.

"That's good," Longarm said. "Now, stay just like that for a minute. . . . "

Rainey had his back to Longarm now and couldn't see the lawman. "What the hell are you doing?" he asked anxiously as he twisted his neck and tried to look back over his shoulder. "What in blazes are you up to, Long?"

Without answering, Longarm walked around the tree and reached underneath his coat. He brought out a pair of handcuffs. Sometimes he kept the cuffs in his saddlebags, but today he'd had them on him, which was another stroke of luck. Otherwise the gray would have carried them off too when he spooked and ran away.

"Stick your arms out," Longarm instructed.

Rainey saw the handcuffs, and his eyes widened as he said, "Aw, hell, Deputy, you can't—"

Longarm lifted the Winchester again.

Rainey bit back a mouthful of profanity and extended his arms. Longarm clapped the cuffs on him with one smooth, practiced movement. Rainey couldn't go anywhere now unless he figured out a way to uproot that post oak and carry it along with him, which Longarm didn't think was very likely. Longarm took a deep breath. He could relax again now, at least for a little while.

"I'll start that bacon frying," he said as he went back toward the horses.

14

"You could've let me take a leak first before you cuffed me to this damn tree," Rainey said.

"Well, I guess having to wait will keep your mind off any mischief you might be thinking about," Longarm replied with a grin.

Over the next few minutes, he ignored Rainey's near-constant complaining and gathered enough small, fallen branches from underneath the trees to make a nice fire in the clearing. Some of the leaves had already fallen with the onset of autumn, and they made good kindling. Longarm had the fire going in no time. He fetched the frying pan from Lloyd's saddlebags and the bacon and already cooked biscuits from Rainey's. Longarm remembered an old trail cook he'd met who claimed his biscuits were the hardest substance known to man, but these would run the old-timer's a close second. They would soften up a mite once they were soaked in some bacon grease, though.

Longarm was kneeling beside the frying pan, listening to the crackle of the bacon and whistling an old cavalry tune about a big black charger and a little white mare, when out of the corner of his eye he caught a flicker of movement downstream. Turning his head to look more closely, he saw the gray gelding he had rented from the stable in Weatherford. The horse was about two hundred yards away, and had emerged from the woods to drink from the stream.

"Well, what do you know?" Longarm said to himself. He stood up and called to his prisoner, "I got to go do something, Rainey. You stay right there."

"Where the hell do you think I'd be going?" the outlaw asked bitterly.

Longarm didn't bother answering. He started walking along the riverbank, moving slowly and on foot so he wouldn't spook the gray again. As the trees grew closer to the edge of the bank, he had to move down into the streambed itself, which was dry along here. The nearest channel of the Brazos was a good fifty yards away. Longarm remembered too late that he'd left the bacon on the fire. It would probably be

15

cooked to a black crisp by the time he got back with the horse, but that couldn't be helped. He could always fry up more bacon. Recovering his saddle and rig was more important.

A bend of the river took him out of sight of Rainey. The Brazos twisted again a little farther downstream, where the gray was still drinking. Once Longarm reached that spot, he would be able to look back upstream and see the place where he had camped with his prisoner. He wasn't worried about Rainey going anywhere, though. Not with his arms around that tree and the handcuffs on his wrists.

Longarm drew steadily closer to the horse. The gray looked up and saw him coming, but didn't seem particularly upset by the sight. That was good, Longarm thought. The horse had settled down since its flight earlier, and that would make it easier to catch. He moved a few steps closer and lifted a hand, reaching out to the gray as he spoke softly and quietly to it, the calming words of a veteran rider who had settled down many a mount. Longarm's fingers were almost touching the reins.

That was when Mitch Rainey started to scream.

Longarm's head jerked around as the shrieks cut through the air. The horse let out a shrill whinny and danced away from him. Longarm said, "Damn!" and lunged after the gray, reaching for the reins. He was too late. The gelding whirled around and raced off into the trees.

Longarm hesitated, torn between going after the horse and finding out what was wrong with Rainey. The prisoner was still screaming—harsh, terrible sounds, as if he was being tortured.

With another curse, Longarm turned and looked upstream. He saw Rainey, still cuffed to the tree, and there was movement beyond the outlaw. The noontime shadows were thick underneath the oaks, so Longarm couldn't tell what was up there that had spooked Rainey so badly. He didn't know if there were any bears left in this part of the country, but there were certainly still plenty of wolves around. Maybe some old lobo had decided that a man cuffed to a tree made a tempting target.

"Hold on, Rainey, I'm coming!" Longarm shouted as he broke into a run toward the clearing. The sandy streambed made for slow going, though, and it seemed to tug hard at his stovepipe cavalry boots with every step he took. As he ran, he drew his pistol and fired it once into the air, hoping the shot might scare off whatever was tormenting Rainey.

The outlaw's cries were fading now, not from any lack of effort on his part, but simply because he had screamed so long and so loud that his throat had to be completely raw by now. He was still making terrified little wheezing noises when Longarm reached him a few moments later.

Longarm peered into the grove of trees, searching intently for whatever had set Rainey to screaming. He didn't see a blessed thing that looked out of the ordinary. Whatever Rainey had spotted up here earlier was gone now. Longarm holstered his gun and looked Rainey over, thinking that maybe the outlaw had been attacked. Other than the dried blood from the bullet crease on his hip, however, there was no sign that Rainey was hurt.

Rainey's eyes were open about as far as humanly possible, and under his tan, his features had an ashen pallor. He kept opening and closing his mouth and uttering small sounds that made no sense. Longarm had heard of people being scared out of their wits before, but Mitch Rainey was probably the only person he'd ever seen who really matched that description.

"What happened here, Rainey?" demanded Longarm. "Why'd you start yelling your fool head off?"

Rainey didn't answer him, didn't even look at him. Instead, Rainey's gaze was still fixed on the spot where Longarm thought he'd seen something moving.

"Damn it, Rainey," Longarm said, angry now because once again he had lost that gray gelding and all the gear that was on the horse. "Tell me what you saw."

Rainey's mouth worked some more, but the sounds that came out were nonsense. Longarm sighed in disgust. Rainey

17

was completely incoherent with fear.

Maybe there were some tracks on the ground, Longarm thought. He went over to the spot Rainey kept staring at and brushed aside some of the leaves that had fallen from the oaks. The ground underneath was fairly soft and took prints well.

Longarm frowned. There were tracks there, all right, but none like he had ever seen before. He hunkered down to get a closer look at them.

At first glance the prints looked like they might have been made by a pair of bare human feet. But even though Longarm had known some old boys with pretty big clodhoppers, he had never seen human feet large enough to make tracks like these. The prints were easily more than twelve inches long. More like fifteen or sixteen, Longarm judged.

It was possible, Longarm supposed, that a fella could grow big enough to have such enormous feet. Some of his previous assignments had taken him to circuses and carnivals, so he was aware that some truly surprising freaks of nature popped up from time to time. But a man couldn't grow pads and claws like a bear on the front of his foot, and for all the world, that was what these tracks looked like: half-man, half-bear.

Suddenly, an eerie cry floated through the air. The sound made Longarm's head snap up, and he felt the skin on the back of his neck prickling. Instinctively, he reached for the butt of his gun. The call had the strangest quality to it Longarm had ever heard. It was almost human, but not quite. On the other hand, it didn't sound like a critter either. It had too much of a man-sound to it for that.

Coldness trickled down Longarm's back like a vagrant drop of winter rain creeping past an oilskin slicker. He was very glad that the cry seemed to come from a good distance away.

Rainey started sobbing.

Longarm took another look at the strange prints and then stood up. He figured Rainey had gotten a good look at whatever had left those tracks and made that sound. Obviously, the thing was enough to spook even a hardened outlaw. Longarm stepped closer to the tree and looked at Rainey's wrists. He hadn't noticed it before, but they were scraped raw and bloody where Rainey had tried unsuccessfully to pull them out of the handcuffs. Rainey had been desperate to get away.

"Don't worry about it, old son," Longarm told the whimpering outlaw. "Whatever it was, it's gone now, and I don't reckon it'll be back. Chances are, it was just as scared of you as you were of it."

Rainey didn't even seem to hear him. The man just kept making sounds like a whipped puppy.

Longarm glanced at the tracks again. He might be able to follow the thing's trail, but he had a prisoner to take care of and the job came first.

At least, that was the way he was going to look at it.

Chapter 3

Just as Longarm had expected, the bacon he'd been frying was nothing but charred little strips of unrecognizable blackness. He didn't care; he had lost his appetite again. If he wanted, he could gnaw on one of those hard biscuits while he was in the saddle, because he was sure of one thing.

He and Rainey were getting the hell out of there.

Rainey's sobs had subsided. The outlaw slumped against the rough bark of the post oak's trunk, his arms wrapped tightly around it as if by holding on to the tree he could also hold on to his sanity. He looked much too shaken to try anything, but Longarm hadn't lived this long by being careless. He unfastened one side of the cuffs and then stepped back quickly, bringing up the Winchester that he had tucked underneath his arm while he freed his prisoner.

Rainey didn't move. He just kept hugging that tree.

Finally, when Rainey didn't respond to the lawman's orders to get mounted, Longarm moved closer and took hold of Rainey's shoulder. He had to practically pry the outlaw away from the tree, and when he did he saw there was a large wet stain on the front of Rainey's trousers. That wasn't a surprise considering how frightened Rainey had been. Besides, he had complained about being cuffed to the tree before he'd had a chance to relieve himself. Longarm felt a little guilty about that now.

But only a little, and the feeling faded even more when he recalled how Rainey and Lloyd had been about to bury him alive only a few hours earlier. He wasn't going to waste perfectly good pity on a hardcase like Rainey. "Come on," he growled. "Either get on that horse and come with me, or I'll leave you here, Rainey."

At last something Longarm said seemed to get through to Rainey's stunned brain. He began shaking his head, and the motion became more vehement, almost violent. He understood the threat, and evidently it was the worst one Longarm could have used. Rainey headed for the chestnut.

The outlaw's arms and legs were trembling, making him awkward as he climbed into the saddle. His eyes darted back and forth constantly as if he expected the horror to reappear at any second. Both of his hands tightly gripped the saddlehorn.

Longarm tossed the burned bacon onto the ground, cleaned the frying pan with sand from the riverbed, then put it away. He swung up onto the Appaloosa and inclined his head to the east. "This looks like as good a place as any to cross the river. Cottonwood Springs can't be more than ten miles the other side of the Brazos."

Rainey paid no attention to him. Longarm grimaced and rode close enough to reach out and take the chestnut's reins. He dallied them around his own saddlehorn for a moment while he refastened the cuff around Rainey's wrist. Rainey didn't put up a fight, didn't even seem to notice what Longarm was doing, in fact. He was too busy looking every which way for whatever had scared him.

For a long moment, Longarm studied the outlaw's face. If there was the slightest chance Rainey was trying to pull some sort of trick so that he could escape, Longarm wanted to nip that hope in the bud. The fear on Rainey's face and in his eyes seemed utterly genuine, though. Longarm shrugged, loosened the chestnut's reins from his saddle and held them, and nudged the Appaloosa into an easy walk.

The bed of the Brazos was almost a hundred yards wide at this point, even though the river itself was much smaller at the moment. Still, the crossing wasn't without its dangers. Closer to the center of the streambed were patches of quicksand that had to be avoided. The water itself was only about eighteen inches deep and the current was sluggish, but again, there were perilous spots where a man and a horse could be pulled down.

Longarm and Rainey reached the eastern side of the river without incident and rode up onto the bank. A ridge ran along this part of the Brazos, with rocky bluffs at the top of the slope overlooking the stream. The climb was fairly steep, but the Appaloosa and the chestnut managed it with no trouble. When they reached the top, some instinct made Longarm rein in and look back over his shoulder. Down below, across the Brazos, he could see the place where he and Rainey had meant to have their noon meal.

Longarm halfway expected to see some sort of monster hunkered there in the clearing, drawn back perhaps by the smell of the burned bacon. But there was nothing, only the peaceful-looking riverbank. Longarm's eyes probed the trees on the far side of the Brazos, but he spotted no movement.

That in itself was a mite strange, he realized with a slight frown. Those oaks should have been full of birds and squirrels. Autumn wasn't so far advanced that all the critters would have headed for their winter homes. At this moment, however, the far side of the river seemed devoid of wildlife.

It was as if the birds and squirrels, which were oftentimes smarter than folks gave them credit for, were hiding out from something that scared them too.

Longarm gave a little shake of his head and turned back to face east. Unless he got completely lost, he and Rainey could make Cottonwood Springs well before dark.

Suddenly, that seemed like an even better idea to Longarm than it had earlier.

Longarm had run into more than his share of strange things over the years. He had tracked the Wendigo, the mythical beast of the Plains Indians, and tangled with murderous mechanical men. His job had put him on the trail of ghosts, grave robbers, mad magicians, and cannibal Indians. He had heard tales as well about the so-called monsters that lurked in the lonely places of the frontier. Some had their source in the stories of the Indians, like the Wendigo and the legendary Sasquatch. Texans had their own yarns, like the one about the monster of Caddo Lake, over in the piney woods of East Texas, and Longarm remembered hearing about a horrible creature that was half-man and half-goat living along the Trinity River northwest of Fort Worth. Then there was Espantosa Lake, down in South Texas, which was supposedly haunted by the ghosts of Spanish conquistadores who had been thrown in by their Indian captors and dragged to their deaths by the weight of their armor.

But those tracks he had found, along with the look on Rainey's face and the way the prisoner was acting, made Longarm feel about as downright creepy as he ever had. He would be glad when they reached Cottonwood Springs and got back among normal folks again.

The farther they traveled away from the Brazos, the better Longarm felt. Rainey calmed down a little too, and stopped twisting his head around so that he could constantly peer in fright over his shoulders. Instead he sat hunched forward in the saddle, his eyes downcast, not paying attention to much of anything. At least he was quiet and not causing any trouble, and Longarm was grateful for small favors.

When Longarm's appetite returned, he took out one of the biscuits and used his pocketknife to cut hunks off it. He had to suck on the pieces of biscuit like they were hard candy for a while before he was able to chew them, but they were surprisingly filling. Rainey didn't nod, shake his head, or even look up when Longarm offered him some of the biscuit. Longarm shrugged. If the outlaw wanted to go hungry, that was

Rainey's lookout. When Longarm was finished with the biscuit, he took a cheroot from his vest pocket and regarded it critically for a moment before putting it in his mouth. The cigar was a little bent from when he had fallen into that grave, but it wasn't broken. He scratched a lucifer into life, held the flame to the tip of the cheroot, and puffed contentedly on it.

Not long after leaving the vicinity of the river, Longarm and Rainey came upon a wagon road that ran east and west. Longarm nudged the Appaloosa onto the trace and headed east, leading the chestnut with Rainey on it. A couple of miles down the trail they reached a crossroad. Wooden signs nailed to a post informed Longarm that the crossroad ran south to Fort Belknap and the town of Graham, while the northbound trail would have taken them to Cimarron Springs and Archer City. To the west, the way they had come, the main road led to Fort Griffin, and to the east, the direction they were headed, lay Cottonwood Springs. Ultimately, Longarm recalled, this road would take them to Jacksboro, Decatur, Boyd's Mill, and Fort Worth. For the time being, however, Longarm would settle for Cottonwood Springs, where he could find a doctor to tend Rainey's wound, then maybe lock the prisoner up in the local jail and enjoy a bath, a hot meal, and a night's sleep in a hotel bed. Longarm sighed in anticipation at the thought.

The rest of the trip to Cottonwood Springs passed without incident. It was after the middle of the afternoon when the two riders came within sight of the settlement. The first things to be visible were the steeples of a pair of churches, one on each end of town. Knowing how folks in this part of the country felt about religion, Longarm was confident that one of the houses of worship was of the Baptist persuasion and the other was likely Methodist. It had always amazed Longarm how people could almost come to blows over whether it was best to be a dunker or a sprinkler. He subscribed to the theory contained in the old hymn ''Farther Along We'll Know More about It,'' so he tended to be tolerant of other folks' beliefs.

As Longarm and Rainey drew closer, the lawman made out more buildings. He hadn't passed through Cottonwood Springs during his wanderings in the past few days, so he wasn't sure how big the town was. It looked to be good-sized, which buoyed Longarm's hopes of finding the place equipped with both a doctor and a sturdy jailhouse. "Come on, Rainey," he said as they reached the point where the wagon road turned into the main street of the town. "Let's get that bullet crease tended to."

"Damn well about time," muttered Rainey, and the outlaw's surly response let Longarm know that Rainey was getting somewhat back to normal. The man had been silent ever since before they had crossed the Brazos.

Longarm hipped around in the saddle to look at Rainey. "You ready to talk about what you saw back there?" Longarm didn't particularly want to bring up the subject, but his curiosity got the best of him.

Rainey shook his head, stone-faced. "Don't know what you're talking about," he said. "I didn't see nothing."

Longarm reined in and frowned. "Hold on there, old son. You mean to tell me you didn't see something that made you start screaming like a banshee?"

"I didn't see a thing," Rainey said stubbornly.

Longarm glowered at the outlaw. "Then why's your voice so hoarse? I'll tell you why—it's from all that yelling you did."

Rainey shook his head.

Longarm took out another cheroot and stuck it in his mouth unlit. His teeth clamped down hard on the cylinder of tobacco. If that was the way Rainey wanted to be about it, fine. What had happened back there at the Brazos didn't have anything to do with Rainey and Lloyd trying to murder him, and it didn't affect the mission that had brought him here, which was to apprehend the pair of outlaws. With a grimace, Longarm turned around and prodded the Appaloosa into a walk.

As he did so, he became aware that there were quite a few people on the streets of Cottonwood Springs, and most of them seemed to be staring at him and his prisoner. The looks on their faces weren't hostile or anything, just . . . surprised,

Longarm decided after a moment. Like they couldn't believe a couple of strangers were riding into town, especially from the west.

Come to think of it, he hadn't seen any other pilgrims on the road this afternoon, Longarm realized, and he would have thought that the road to Fort Griffin would be a well-traveled route. An uneasy sensation prickled along his spine again.

There were no boardwalks in Cottonwood Springs, but several of the businesses had elevated porches built onto the front of the buildings. Longarm veered the Appaloosa toward a hotel called the Cottonwood House. As usual for a small town, several elderly men were sitting on cane-bottomed chairs on the hotel's porch. Longarm brought the horses to a stop by the hitch rack and nodded to the loafers. "Afternoon, gentlemen," he said. "Can one of you tell me whereabouts I might find the local law?"

The old-timers just stared at him and didn't say anything.

Longarm swallowed his irritation and impatience. "You *do* have a sheriff or a marshal here in Cottonwood Springs, don't you?"

One of the men finally said something, even though it wasn't an answer to either of Longarm's questions. "You come here from somewhere around the Brazos, stranger?"

"That's right. The other side of the river, in fact."

Two more of the old men looked at each other, and one of them said, "He crossed the Brazos." From the tone of his voice, Longarm might just as well have hopped down to Texas from the moon.

This time Longarm couldn't contain his reaction. He snapped, "Look, I'm a deputy United States marshal. Have you got any law around here or not?"

The first old-timer who had spoken huffed up and said, "No call to get all peevish, mister. If you were lookin' for Mal Burley, why didn't you just say so?"

Longarm gritted his teeth and refrained from pointing out that he had done that very thing a few seconds earlier.

"You'll find Mal down at the bank," the old man said,

pointing to a substantial brick building about a block away. "I wouldn't bother him right now, though. He's talkin' to Mr. Thorp."

Longarm didn't know or care who Mr. Thorp was, but he didn't waste his time or breath saying so. He just nodded to the codger, grunted "Thanks," and headed the Appaloosa toward the bank, leading the chestnut behind him.

Before he could reach the bank, Longarm spotted a man wearing a star pinned to his vest emerging from the brick building. In contrast to his name, Mal Burley was short, slender, and narrow-shouldered. Most small-town lawmen relied on brawn to get their jobs done, but Burley wouldn't have that luxury. On the other hand, Cottonwood Springs looked like the sort of place that was fairly peaceful most of the time, even though for some reason there *were* a lot of people in town at the moment.

Another man followed Burley out of the bank. He wore a town suit, but his boots and Stetson were those of a rancher. He was medium-sized—which still made him bigger than the local marshal—and had graying dark hair. His clean-shaven face wore a belligerent expression.

Longarm was already within earshot as the local lawman swung around and said to the man following him, "I told you, Mr. Thorp, I'm doing everything I can. You said you wanted reports every day, and it's not my fault that there's nothing new to tell you."

"It's been three weeks, Mal," Thorp said. "You can't blame me for being worried."

"No, sir, I sure can't," agreed Burley. "But I can't change the way things are either."

Thorp's mouth tightened. "Maybe it's time *I* made a change."

For a moment, Burley didn't say anything. Then he nodded curtly and said, "You do whatever you have to do, Mr. Thorp."

"I always do."

This exchange was interesting as all get out, Longarm

27

thought as he reined up in front of the bank, but it didn't have a damned thing to do with him. He cleared his throat and said, "Marshal Burley?"

Both Burley and Thorp looked up at him in surprise. They had been so wrapped up in their own conversation they hadn't seen him approaching with his prisoner. Burley asked, "What can I do for you, mister?"

"Name's Custis Long. I'm a deputy United States marshal out of Denver, and this is a federal prisoner I have with me. I was wondering if I might take advantage of your hospitality and put him in your lockup for a spell. He needs a doctor to look at him too."

"A federal badge, eh?" Burley said, clearly a little annoyed at the interruption but interested and impressed in spite of himself.

"That's right. I've got my bona fides right here." Longarm reached under his coat and took from an inner pocket the small leather folder which contained his badge and identification papers. He handed them to Burley, having to lean over in the saddle to do so because of the man's short stature. Burley studied the badge for a moment, and as he did Thorp was also examining it over his shoulder.

"Looks like you're the genuine article, Marshal Long," Burley said as he handed the folder back to Longarm. "You can leave your prisoner in my jail for as long as you like. I don't get too many customers in Cottonwood Springs. Not likely we'll run out of room. I'll send word for Doc Carson to come down there, if that's all right."

"Much obliged."

"Who have you got there?"

"His name's Mitch Rainey," Longarm said. "He and his partner have been holding up stages hereabouts."

Burley let out a low whistle. "You caught up to Rainey and Lloyd?" He sounded impressed.

Longarm didn't want to point out that it hadn't been all that difficult of a chore, when it had obviously proved too much for this local lawman. He merely shrugged and jerked a thumb

28

over his shoulder toward the prisoner. "There's half of 'em."

"Where's Lloyd?"

"In a shallow grave about twenty miles a little north by west from here."

Thorp stepped forward, suddenly showing even more interest. "That's on the other side of the Brazos."

"Yes, sir, it is," Longarm agreed. "We crossed the river along about noon."

Thorp reached out, grabbing hold of the Appaloosa's bridle. "Did you see it, man?" he demanded in a shaky voice. "Did you see it?"

Longarm wasn't sure he wanted to hear the answer, but he asked the question anyway. "See what?"

"The Brazos Devil!"

Chapter 4

Longarm hesitated, unsure how to respond to the man. He looked over at Marshal Mal Burley, but didn't get any clue from the diminutive lawman. Longarm had a pretty good idea what Thorp was talking about, but he didn't know how much he wanted to say about the incident beside the river earlier in the day.

He was saved from having to say anything by the pitiful whimper Rainey suddenly let out. The outlaw might have been almost back to normal when they entered town, but now he was hunched over in his saddle again and that terrified, furtive look had returned to his eyes. His breath hissed between tightly clenched teeth.

Thorp turned toward him. "You *have* seen it!" he exclaimed. "You must have! Was there a woman with it?"

The man's excitement was drawing a crowd, and Longarm heard the murmured comments that leaped from bystander to bystander. "The strangers had a run-in with the Brazos Devil!" one man said. Variations on that theme filled the air.

"Maybe we'd better go on over to your jail," Longarm suggested to Burley as he put away his cheroot still unlit. "Then you can tell me what's going on here."

"Not a bad idea," Burley said. He lifted his arms and raised his voice as he addressed the gathering crowd, and the words boomed out with a surprising resonance for a man of his size. "Just on about your business, folks! This is nothing to do with the Brazos Devil!"

Nobody seemed to believe him, but the crowd parted to let Longarm, Rainey, and Burley through as they headed for the jail. Thorp strode along right behind them as if he belonged, and for all Longarm knew, he did. Maybe he was the mayor of Cottonwood Springs; Longarm just didn't know.

He didn't know anything about a creature called the Brazos Devil either, but he could make a reasonable guess. The people in this area had themselves a local legend, and judging by its name, the Brazos Devil was some sort of monster, like the Wendigo, Sasquatch, the Caddo Critter, and that Goatman.

Well, Rainey had seen *something,* whether he denied it now or not, and something had made those tracks Longarm had found near the river. It had been his experience that things supernatural always turned out to have some logical, reasonable explanation.

But there was always a first time. . . .

The crowd trailed along behind Longarm and his companions, and stood around chattering excitedly while Longarm dismounted and hauled Rainey down from the chestnut's saddle. Marshal Burley took the reins and looped them around the hitch rack in front of the jailhouse made from blocks of native stone. After sending one of the bystanders down the street to fetch the doctor, he led the way inside and the crowd stopped short of entering—all but Thorp, that is. He shut the door behind them and said urgently, "Was there a woman with the creature?"

Longarm ignored the question for the time being. He took hold of Rainey's arm and pulled the outlaw across the small office in the front of the jail toward a heavy wooden door with a small barred window set in it. Longarm knew from experience that such a door always led to the cell block. Burley went first, using a key from a large ring to open the cell-block door.

The cells on the other side were all vacant, their doors standing open. Longarm took Rainey to the closest one and shoved him, not too roughly, through the door. He slammed it shut with a clang.

Rainey was quaking like an aspen. He sank down on the cell's hard bunk and drew his legs up beside him, curling himself into a ball. He seemed to relax a little then, as if the knowledge that he was locked in a cell made him feel better instead of worse. Rainey might be locked away from everything, Longarm thought—but everything was also locked away from Rainey.

Thorp came into the cell block. "Well, what about it?" he said harshly. "For God's sake, tell me what you saw out there!"

"I'm getting a mite tired of your tone of voice, mister," Longarm said. "Hell, we haven't even been introduced yet, and you're already full of questions."

Thorp's eyes widened as if no one ever talked to him that way, and Burley stepped smoothly between him and Longarm. "This is Mr. Benjamin Thorp, Marshal," the local star-packer said, "owner of the Bank of Cottonwood Springs and the Rocking T ranch."

"And the richest man in town," Longarm guessed.

"I don't give a damn about money right now," Thorp said. "I just want my wife back. Did you see her or not?"

"I didn't see anything," Longarm said, "but I wish one of you fellas would tell me what this is all about."

Thorp opened his mouth to speak again, but Burley stopped him by saying, "Come back out into the office with me, Marshal Long, and I'll explain the whole thing. Maybe you can suggest something I haven't thought of."

Longarm couldn't tell about that until he knew what was going on. He followed Burley from the cell block into the office, and Benjamin Thorp brought up the rear.

Burley went behind an old desk with a scarred wooden top and gestured toward a chair in front of the desk. The chair was padded with black leather. Longarm sat down, propped his right ankle on his left knee, and took off his hat, dropping it on the floor beside him. Burley settled himself on a chair behind the desk, and since the seat was out of sight, Longarm wondered idly if the local lawman had boosted it with a couple of books or something. Burley seemed taller sitting down. Another of the padded chairs like the one Longarm was sitting in was against the wall of the small room, but Thorp didn't take it. Instead he started pacing back and forth.

Burley said, "I'd tell you to take it easy, Mr. Thorp, but I know it wouldn't do any good."

"Damned right it wouldn't," growled Thorp. "I'm not going to relax until my wife is back with me, safe and sound! Hell, how can you expect a man to take it easy when the women he loves has been dragged off by some unholy monster!"

Burley held up a hand. "You go right ahead and pace," he said, "while I tell Marshal Long what happened."

Longarm took that cheroot from his pocket again. "Reckon I can guess some of it," he said as he struck a match with a flick of his iron-hard thumbnail. "Mrs. Thorp is missing, and for some reason you folks think she was carried off by a critter called the Brazos Devil."

"I thought you said you hadn't seen it," Thorp snapped.

"I haven't."

"Then how did you know—"

"I've got eyes and ears," Longarm said patiently. "And ever since Rainey and I rode into Cottonwood Springs a little while ago, folks have been acting pretty worked up about something. I just listened and put it all together."

Burley leaned back in his chair and asked, "Had you ever heard of the Brazos Devil before today, Marshal?"

Longarm took a puff on the cheroot and shook his head. "Nope. But I've heard other local legends that I'd be willing to bet are similar. This here Brazos Devil—he's some sort of hairy half-man, half-monster, right?"

"That's what the people who have seen him say," Burley

admitted. "They claim he's about seven feet tall and covered with fur."

"Anybody ever stop to think that maybe it's a bear?" asked Longarm as he remembered those prints he had seen in the soft dirt. He didn't want to mention them just yet.

"Well, in the first place, there aren't any bears in these parts. There probably aren't any bears in Texas this side of the Big Bend. And for another thing, people have seen it run, and it doesn't run like a bear. It runs like a man."

"Folks have seen it close up, have they?" Longarm was still skeptical, but he was curious enough about this matter to forgo that hot meal and bath and hotel room for a while.

"Not too close," Burley said with a shrug. "But close enough to tell that it wasn't like anything they'd ever seen before." He sighed and added grimly, "I'm afraid the only ones who have gotten a really good look at the Brazos Devil can't tell us anything about it."

"Too afraid?" Longarm asked, thinking about Rainey's reaction and the stunned silence that had gripped the outlaw for most of the afternoon.

"Too dead," Burley said.

"Damn it, Mal!" Thorp burst out miserably. "You know that thing's got Emmaline!"

Burley grimaced and leaned forward. "Sorry, Mr. Thorp. I guess I wasn't thinking. I didn't mean to upset you even more."

Longarm had a feeling Thorp, as the town's leading citizen, must have installed Burley in the marshal's job, either directly or through his influence. But Longarm didn't depend on the banker and rancher for his livelihood, so he said bluntly, "You're saying this Brazos Devil has killed folks?"

"Four that we know of, including Matt Hardcastle, Mr. Thorp's foreman. Matt was killed when the thing ran off with Mrs. Thorp."

Longarm blew out another cloud of blue smoke. "Back up a mite and tell me about that."

"I don't know," Burley said. "Maybe Mr. Thorp . . ."

Thorp took off his hat, ran a hand over his thinning hair, then breathed deeply and put a look of resolve on his face. "It hurts to talk about it," he said, "but if there's a chance you might be able to help us, Marshal Long, I suppose I can bring myself to do it."

"I can't promise anything," Longarm said mildly, "but I'm willing to listen."

"All right. About three weeks ago, my wife went out for a ride on our ranch. It's her habit to go riding several times a week."

"Horseback riding, you mean? Not in a buggy?" Longarm interrupted to ask.

Thorp nodded. "That's right. Emmaline is very fond of it and is actually a good horsewoman. She grew up in Louisiana, and she never got a chance to ride horses when she was a child. I go with her whenever I can, but my business keeps me either at the ranch house or here in town most of the time."

"So you sent your foreman, this fella Hardcastle, with her whenever you couldn't go," Longarm ventured.

"Yes. Especially after what happened to the Lavery boys."

Longarm looked at Burley, and the marshal said, "Howard Lavery's three sons. The Laverys have a little spread southwest of here, and the boys were found dead on the road about six weeks ago."

"Killed?" Longarm asked.

Burley nodded, his narrow features bleak. "Torn all to pieces, in fact. It like to've turned my stomach. Something ripped those fellas apart with its bare hands. There hasn't been too much traffic on the road since then."

Thorp shuddered and lifted a hand, covering his face for a moment. He took a deep breath and went on. "After that, I tried to persuade Emmaline that her horseback rides weren't a good idea, but she wouldn't hear of giving them up." He gave a little shrug. "You don't know Emmaline, Marshal, but there's no arguing with her when she gets something in her head. She insisted she was perfectly safe as long as Matt or I was with her."

35

"But she wasn't," Longarm said heavily.

Thorp clearly had to force himself to go on. "Matt's horse came back alone to the ranch. There . . . there was blood on the saddle. The men sent word to me in town immediately, and also started a search party on the horse's backtrail. By the time I got to the ranch and caught up with them, they . . . they had found Matt's . . . body."

"He was torn up just like the Lavery boys," Burley put in. "But there was no sign of Mrs. Thorp or her horse, so it could be she got away from whatever attacked Hardcastle."

"That was three weeks ago, Mal!" exclaimed Thorp. "If Emmaline was all right, why hasn't she come home by now?"

"Maybe what she saw scared her so bad she hasn't stopped running yet," Longarm suggested. "I've heard of folks who had such a shock that they clean forgot who they were."

Thorp frowned and said, "That's mighty unlikely, don't you think, Deputy?"

No more so than jumping to the conclusion that Emmaline Thorp had been dragged off by a monster, Longarm thought, but he kept that to himself and merely shrugged. He said, "I don't know the lady. You tell me, Mr. Thorp."

Thorp shook his head decisively. "No, that wouldn't happen. Emmaline is too levelheaded to completely lose her wits just because she was frightened. The only reason she wouldn't come back to the ranch house is if she *couldn't*."

Before the discussion could continue, the office door opened and a heavyset man carrying a black medical bag came in. He had jowls like a bulldog and was wide across the shoulders, but his hands were surprisingly small, almost delicate. He nodded to Thorp and Longarm, then said to Burley, "I hear you've got a patient for me, Mal."

"I'll take you back to him, Doc," Burley said as he stood up and reached for the key ring.

"The fella's got a bullet crease on his right hip," Longarm offered. "It never bled much, so I don't figure it amounts to anything."

Doc Carson nodded. "Doubtless you're correct, sir, but the

wound should still be examined and cleaned.''

Burley opened the heavy door and took the physician into the cell block. Longarm smoked in silence and Thorp paced until Burley returned, leaving the cell-block door open this time.

As the local lawman settled himself behind the desk again, Longarm asked, "Did Mrs. Thorp's horse leave any tracks you could follow?"

"Matt's body was found on a rocky outcropping over the river," Thorp said. "The ground was too hard to take tracks."

"What about in the rest of the area? Any hoofprints or . . . anything else?"

If Thorp or Burley noticed the slight pause, neither man gave any sign of it. Burley shook his head and said, "There had been too many riders milling around there, what with the search party and everything. There weren't any tracks that meant anything."

"Where'd this happen?"

"Like I said, it was on one of the bluffs overlooking the river on my ranch," replied Thorp. "My spread runs from the Fort Griffin road north for about fifteen miles along the east side of the Brazos."

Longarm considered that for a moment as he smoked. "That means Rainey and I were on your land when we came across the river today."

"That's right, but I don't worry about people crossing my spread. The northern boundary and part of the eastern boundary are fenced to keep my stock from wandering too much, but otherwise it's all open range. The river forms a natural barrier to the west."

"Then the place where Hardcastle's body was found probably wasn't very far from where Rainey and I came across."

"Describe the spot to me," Thorp suggested. Longarm did so, and the rancher nodded. "That's about two miles north of where Matt's body was found," he said. His features were taut with repressed anger and anxiety as he went on. "I've been patient, Long. That outlaw you brought in obviously saw *something* out there. Don't you think under the circumstances you ought to tell us about it?"

The man had a point, Longarm had to give him that. Quickly, he told Thorp and Burley about the incident beside the river, even describing the mysterious footprints this time. Thorp became even more agitated and excited as Longarm talked, and Burley leaned forward eagerly.

"Rainey had to have seen the Brazos Devil!" Thorp said when Longarm was finished. "That's the only explanation that makes any sense!"

"And those tracks you saw sound like the same ones we found around the bodies of the Lavery boys," Burley put in. "It must've been the creature."

"Hold on a minute," Longarm said with a stubborn frown. "I don't know if I'm willing to just assume such a critter even exists."

"How can you doubt it?" demanded Thorp. "Look at all the evidence!"

"That's what I'm trying to do—"

Longarm was saved from further arguing by the reappearance of the doctor. Carson was closing his bag as he came out of the cell block. "You were right, sir," he said to Longarm. "The wound on the patient's hip is superficial. He'll be bruised and sore for a few days, but there won't be any lasting effects." Carson hesitated, then added, "I'm more concerned about the man's, ah, mental state."

"He hasn't calmed down any?" Longarm asked.

"He's well nigh catatonic. That means—"

"I know what it means," Longarm said. "He's so shaken up about something that he's pulled back into himself and ain't letting anybody else in."

"Exactly," agreed the physician.

"What are the chances of making him talk, Doc?" asked Thorp.

Carson shook his head. "Hard to say. Cases like this where the patient has suffered a great shock are almost impossible to predict."

"He seemed to be coming around earlier," Longarm said, "until he got reminded again of what happened out there."

"Then that's a good sign. With time, he may make a full recovery." Carson shrugged. "Or maybe not."

Thorp took a step toward the cell-block door. "Well, he'll just have to come out of it, because I've got to talk to him!"

Carson put a hand out to stop him. "Sorry, Mr. Thorp, but it won't do you any good to browbeat the man, especially now. I gave him a sedative since he seemed so disturbed. He's sound asleep by now."

"Damn it, Carson!" Thorp burst out. "You didn't have the right—"

"The man is my patient. I had the right to make a medical judgment, and I did so."

Longarm also wished the doctor hadn't knocked Rainey out, but it was too late now to do anything about it. He said, "There's no sense in getting upset, Thorp. Rainey'll wake up sooner or later, and you and the marshal can talk to him then."

"Yes, and in the meantime that monster has even more time to put my wife through the tortures of hell!"

"We don't know that Mrs. Thorp is in any danger," Burley said. "Maybe the Devil's just sort of . . . holding her prisoner."

The withering look Thorp gave Burley made it clear just how likely the rancher considered that possibility.

As for Longarm, he wondered why the creature—assuming that the Brazos Devil even existed, and that was a mighty big assumption—would carry off a woman when its other encounters with men had proven fatal. There was only one reason Longarm could think of, and it was a horrifying prospect that had no doubt occurred to Thorp, Burley, and everybody else in Cottonwood Springs.

Maybe the monster had wanted a mate. . . .

Longarm put that image out of his mind with a little shake of his head. He still had his own job to tend to, and something else had occurred to him. He said, "Mr. Thorp, you reckon I could use the safe in your bank to lock up some valuables overnight?"

"Of course," Thorp replied with a wave of his hand, obviously distracted and a bit put out by the question.

Longarm put his hand inside his coat. "Unless, that is, one of you gents happens to know who these baubles belong to so that I can get 'em back to their rightful owner?" He took out the necklace and bracelet he had found in Rainey's saddlebag.

He should have figured it out sooner, he realized immediately. But all it took was the strangled sound Thorp made, the widening of the man's eyes, and the heartfelt curse that came from Burley's lips. "Where did you get those?" the marshal asked hoarsely.

Longarm sat forward, his muscles tense. "You're saying they belong to—"

"They belong to my wife!" Thorp said in a voice that was almost a wail. "That's Emmaline's jewelry!"

Chapter 5

Longarm stared at the man for a second, then asked, "Was she wearing these things when she disappeared?"

Thorp seemed to have aged another year or so in the moment since he had seen the shiny necklace and bracelet in Longarm's hand. He nodded without saying anything.

"Your wife wore geegaws like this to go horseback riding on a ranch?" Longarm asked with a frown.

"I told you she was raised in Louisiana," Thorp said. "New Orleans, to be exact. She always liked nice things. She said that . . . just because she was living on a ranch was no reason not to . . . to enjoy her jewelry."

Thorp appeared to be on the verge of breaking down. Carson moved to his side and said solicitously, "Maybe I ought to give you something too, Mr. Thorp."

Thorp pulled away from the doctor and shook his head vigorously. "I don't want anything," he said. "I have to be able to think clearly."

It might be a little too late for that, Longarm figured. Thorp seemed about one step away from losing his mind, and Longarm supposed he couldn't blame the man for that. He himself didn't want to start believing in monsters, but *something* had happened to Emmaline Thorp, and the overwhelming odds were that it was bad.

Longarm stood up and handed the jewelry to Thorp. "I reckon you'd better take care of these," he said. "Your wife'll want 'em when she gets back."

Thorp nodded numbly. "Where did you get them?"

Longarm inclined his head toward the cell-block door. "Rainey had them in his saddlebags."

"Then . . . maybe he and his partner had Emmaline—" Thorp wheeled and lunged toward the cell block. "I'll kill him!"

Longarm's hand shot out and clamped down on Thorp's arm, jerking the rancher to a stop. Burley was already up and moving, putting himself between Thorp and the cell block. "Hold on there!" Longarm said in a hard voice. "I already thought of what you're thinking, Thorp, and I got to admit you might be right."

"Are you saying Rainey and Lloyd killed Matt Hardcastle instead of the Brazos Devil?" asked Burley.

Longarm shrugged. "I'm not saying anything. But even if . . . something else . . . killed Hardcastle, Mrs. Thorp could've been running away from whatever it was when she bumped into those two outlaws."

If that was the case, it was possible, even likely, that a couple of hardcases like Rainey and Lloyd would have raped her. And if she'd put up a fight, one of them could have hit her too hard. . . .

It was a plausible explanation. Just because Rainey and Lloyd hadn't killed anybody that Longarm knew of didn't mean he could put rape and murder past them. They had certainly been quick enough to try to kill *him,* and in a particularly cruel and gruesome fashion at that.

"Rainey's knocked out right now," Longarm said. "When he wakes up, we'll question him."

"*If* he's coherent again," Doc Carson put in.

"He'll be coherent enough to answer our questions," Thorp

42

said coldly. "If he wants to live to see another sunrise, he'll answer us."

Longarm refrained from pointing out that Rainey was a federal prisoner. He wasn't about to let Thorp or anybody else kill a prisoner in his charge.

But Longarm wanted to get to the bottom of this mess too, and the best place to start would be by questioning Rainey when he regained his senses.

In the meantime, he was long overdue for that bath and a hot meal. He looked at Burley and said, "I'm leaving Rainey in your custody, Marshal. I expect nothing'll happen to him while I go clean up and get myself a meal."

Burley nodded curtly. "Nobody will bother the prisoner, Deputy Long. You've got my word on that." He looked meaningfully at Thorp.

The rancher seemed to have recovered his own senses a little. He said, "Don't worry, Long. Right now, the man in that cell block is worth even more to me than he is to you." Thorp looked at the heavy wooden door and drew a deep breath. "He's going to tell me what happened to my wife."

Rainey slept through the night as the sedative Carson had given him did its work, and he was surprisingly lucid the next morning. Longarm was on hand when Burley and Thorp questioned the outlaw. He was feeling considerably more human himself after a night's sleep and a hearty breakfast. He would have felt even better, Longarm reflected, if his slumber hadn't been haunted by images of giant hairy creatures that ran like men.

Rainey shook his head stubbornly to every question Burley and Thorp threw at him. "I didn't see nothin' out there," he insisted. "And I sure as hell didn't see your wife, mister. Jimmy and me, we never laid a hand on her, 'cause we didn't run into her."

"What about this jewelry?" asked Thorp as he held up the necklace and bracelet.

Rainey's eyes lit up with avarice at the sight of the jewelry,

43

but the reaction was fleeting. He became sullen again and said, "Like I told Long, we found that stuff on the trail."

"Found it," repeated Burley.

"That's right, damn it! And we picked it up too. Would *you* ride away and leave something like that laying on the ground?"

Thorp growled, "And we're supposed to take the word of a holdup man that that's what happened." He snorted in contempt.

Thorp was more in control of himself this morning, Longarm noted. The man was still upset, of course, and hollow-eyed from lack of sleep. But the rage that had gripped him the day before seemed to have subsided. That made the questioning easier, if not more fruitful.

"Listen, Rainey," Longarm put in from his position leaning against the bars of the opposite cell, his arms crossed over his chest, "you'll make it easier on yourself if you tell us the truth."

"I am telling the truth, damn it! Can't any of you get that through your head? I'm already behind bars! What in blazes do I have to gain by lying?"

"Right now you're facing federal charges of stealing Uncle Sam's mail and assault and attempted murder of a deputy marshal, namely me," Longarm told him. "That'll land you in Leavenworth for a fair number of years, but if you behave yourself I reckon you got a good chance of coming out alive." Longarm's voice grew quieter and more menacing. "But if you and your late pard had anything to do with Mrs. Thorp's disappearance, old son, I don't reckon you'll live to see Denver, let alone Leavenworth. I might just ride off and let these good folks here in Cottonwood Springs have you. So if you know anything at all about Mrs. Thorp, you'd be smart to tell us."

Truth to tell, Longarm didn't know what he would do if Rainey confessed to murdering Emmaline Thorp. He had already lost Lloyd; he didn't want to lose the remaining bandit too. But he couldn't in all good conscience deny Texas law

44

the opportunity to deal with a killer. Not to mention the fact that if he tried to take Rainey away under those circumstances, *he* might wind up on the wrong end of a lynch rope too.

It didn't come to that. Rainey looked from Longarm to Burley to Thorp, and he said miserably, "I swear, gents, I never saw any woman over there on the other side of the Brazos. Jimmy and me *found* that jewelry, just like I said, and I'll swear to that on as big a stack of bibles as you want to pile up."

Thorp glared at him for a moment, then grabbed the bars of the cell so tightly that his knuckles turned white. "You're lying!" he hissed between his teeth. "Burley, let me in there with him for five minutes! By God, I'll have the truth out of him!"

Rainey was sitting on the bunk. He cringed back against the wall and pointed a finger at Thorp. "You can't do that, Marshal!" he yelled at Burley. "You keep that crazy man away from me! It ain't fittin' that he's even in here."

Burley put a hand on Thorp's arm. "Come on, Mr. Thorp. We're just wasting our time here. Let's go out in the office and talk about it."

"We've been talking for three weeks, goddamn it! None of it has brought my wife back! I'm tired of talking!"

Longarm got on Thorp's other side, and he and Burley were able to steer the upset rancher out of the cell block. Thorp went reluctantly, and he spat curses back over his shoulder at Rainey as the two lawmen led him out.

Longarm felt a little relieved when the cell-block door was closed and locked. Thorp was damned near frothing at the mouth by this time, and Longarm supposed he couldn't blame him. He and Burley got Thorp settled down in the chair in front of the desk.

Burley looked at Longarm and asked, "What do you think, Long? Is Rainey telling the truth?"

Longarm rubbed a thumbnail along his freshly shaven jaw and then tugged on his right earlobe in thought. "I think he is," he finally said.

45

"That's insane!" Thorp exploded. "He has to be lying!"

"He's still pretty shook up after that scare he had yesterday," Longarm said, "and he knows how much trouble he's in here. If he and Lloyd *did* have anything to do with your wife's disappearance, I think he'd lie about it, all right, but he wouldn't just dummy up like that. His sort usually starts trying to spin some fancy yarn to take them off the hook, and that's what trips 'em up. When you're dealing with owlhoots like Rainey, a good rule of thumb is the simpler the story, the more likely it is to be true."

Thorp shook his head. "I still don't believe him." He glowered at Longarm. "And you're not going to take him back to Denver when he may be the key to finding my wife either!"

Longarm had done some debating with himself on that very subject. He had been gone from Denver long enough already, and it was time to be getting back with his prisoner. On the other hand, he couldn't blame Burley and Thorp for wanting to keep Rainey here in Cottonwood Springs until the matter of Emmaline Thorp's disappearance was settled. He had come up with a compromise, and he said now, "I don't intend to move on right away, especially since I noticed you've got a Western Union office here. I'll send a wire to my boss to let him know that Lloyd's dead and Rainey is in custody, but I'll tell him we'll be delayed for a few days at the request of the local authorities. That ought to placate Billy . . . for a while."

"Thanks, Long," Burley said. "I'm glad you're cooperating. I don't have any desire to get in a ruckus with the U.S. government."

Thorp stood up. "You two can throw bouquets at each other all you want. I'm going back in there and question that owlhoot some more."

Before Longarm or Burley could say anything, the door of the marshal's office opened, and a tall, thin young man in a suit and a stiff collar came in and said, "Mr. Thorp, I think you'd better get over to the bank right away."

"What the hell's wrong, Stanley?" Thorp asked, not bothering to conceal his irritation. He kept staring at the cell block

46

door, as if he could see something on the other side of it.

The young man swallowed hard and said, "There are some . . . people there to see you. One of them said to tell you his name was Booth."

Thorp's head jerked around. "Booth?" he repeated. "My God, I didn't expect him so soon."

Burley said worriedly, "What's going on here, Mr. Thorp? Who's this fella Booth?"

Thorp ignored him. He stalked over to the door, seemingly galvanized by the news his assistant had brought. "Thanks, Stanley," he said. He went out, trailed by the young man.

Longarm and Burley exchanged a glance. Burley didn't like this, and Longarm's instincts told him it could be more trouble too. Acting as if with one mind, both men started toward the door.

A crowd had already started gathering in front of the bank, Longarm saw as he and Burley emerged from the marshal's office. And with good reason, because the people standing on the porch in front of the bank were like nothing the good citizens of Cottonwood Springs had ever seen before.

The man and the woman standing together were normal enough, Longarm saw as he and Burley drew closer. Thorp had already reached the bank and was shaking hands with the man, who wore a fringed buckskin coat, a big cream-colored Stetson, tight brown trousers, and high-topped black boots. It was the sort of outfit one of those Wild West Show impresarios back East would wear, Longarm thought. The gent was tall and lean and had a dark spade beard.

The woman was dressed more elegantly, her gown the height of fashion even though it was a little dusty at the moment, no doubt from riding in one of the wagons that were parked in front of the bank. Longarm put her age around thirty, which made her about fifteen years younger than the man she was with. She had dark red hair under a feathered hat, and she was undeniably beautiful.

Their two companions were the ones attracting most of the attention from the townspeople. One of the men was tall and broad-shouldered and had a turban of some sort that came to a point on top wrapped around his head. His beard stuck out in two tufts, one on each side of his chin, and his face was the color of saddle leather. He wore boots and loose trousers and a tunic with a broad leather sash tied around his waist. Tucked behind that sash was a wicked-looking sword with a wide, curving blade. He was armed as well with a rifle equipped with a sling, which he carried over one shoulder. Longarm didn't recognize the rifle and wondered if it was of foreign manufacture, because the gent carrying it sure as hell was.

The other man also wore a turban, and his tunic came almost to his knees. He was as dark-skinned as his partner but clean-shaven, and he wasn't armed as far as Longarm could tell. He was also about half the size of the man standing next to him on the porch of the bank. From Longarm's reading in the Denver Public Library on those days close to the end of the month when he'd run out of drinking and gambling money, Longarm recognized both of them as being from India or some such Asian country.

The wagons that had evidently brought the foursome to Cottonwood Springs were ordinary, medium-sized vehicles with canvas coverings over their beds, the type of wagons that could be bought or rented at practically any wagon yard. The teams hitched to them were good enough, Longarm saw, running his eyes over them as would any experienced judge of horseflesh, but like the wagons they pulled, they were quite common. It was the people who had arrived in these conveyances who were out of the ordinary.

Burley stepped up onto the porch and asked bluntly, "Who's this, Mr. Thorp?"

"The man who's going to find my wife," Thorp said. "The man who's going to track down the Brazos Devil and kill it once and for all. Marshal Burley, this is John Booth, Lord Beechmuir, and his wife Lady Beechmuir."

"How do you do, Marshal?" John Booth said to Burley in a strong British accent. He extended a hand, which the local

48

lawman shook a little dubiously. "It's quite an honor to be here in your community. Quite an honor indeed to be asked to hunt down this bloody beast that's been plaguing you and your citizens, eh, what?"

Thorp was excited. He had forgotten for the moment about Rainey, Longarm saw, and was worked up again about the Brazos Devil. He turned to Longarm and Burley and said, "I read in the newspaper that Lord Beechmuir was in San Antonio on a visit, and I figured he'd be the perfect man for the job. After all, he's hunted big game all over the world, haven't you, Lord Beechmuir?"

"Indeed," said the Englishman. "Elephants in Africa, tigers in India . . . you name it and I've shot it." He moved slightly aside. "Allow me to introduce my wife. Helene, this is Mr. Benjamin Thorp, our host."

Helene Booth murmured a properly demure greeting and shook hands with Thorp, although she looked as if she halfway expected him to kiss her hand instead of shake it. As she turned away, her eyes met Longarm's for an instant, and he felt as if somebody had just punched him in the belly. There was something incredibly powerful about Helene's gaze, something raw and primordial that called out to the male animal residing deep within Longarm, the atavistic savage that dwelled inside all men.

"Lordy," he muttered to himself, sweeping those thoughts away with an effort. Unless he missed his guess, Helene Booth was one damned horny woman.

". . . my servants, Absalom Singh and Randamar Ghote," Booth was saying. Singh was the tall one with the sword and the beard, judging by the way he bowed when Booth said the name. That would make Ghote the little one, and Longarm wondered idly if anybody had ever called him Billy.

"There have been some unexpected developments, Lord Beechmuir," Thorp said, "but I still want you to try to track down the creature we think may be out there somewhere along the Brazos. We still can't rule out the possibility that it exists, and that it took my wife."

"Please, call me John," Booth replied. "And you can be assured that I shall do my utmost to rescue your lovely bride, Benjamin. The head of this Brazos Devil of yours will make quite the trophy for the wall of my club back in London, eh?"

Longarm felt almost as if he had stepped into the middle of some opera house play without knowing it. He wished for a second he had headed for Graham or Palo Pinto or some other town instead of Cottonwood Springs. He had a job to do, and the presence of an English big-game hunter, his overheated redheaded wife, and a couple of turban-wearing Indians of the subcontinent sort would just complicate things.

He was about to find out just how much of a complication, because Booth went on. "I believe this is one hunt I would make even without that twenty-thousand-dollar bounty you're offering, Benjamin."

Chapter 6

"Bounty?" Marshal Burley repeated. "Did you say something about a bounty, Mr. Booth?"

"That's correct," the Englishman said. "Twenty thousand dollars for the head of the Brazos Devil." He added to Thorp, "Quite sporting of you, Benjamin, I must say."

Burley turned to Thorp and said in an accusing tone, "You didn't tell me anything about a bounty, Mr. Thorp."

"Well, it's none of your business," snapped the rancher, looking not the least bit repentant. "After more than a week had gone by and you hadn't found any sign of Emmaline, I knew I had to do *something*."

Longarm knew what Burley was worried about, and the local lawman confirmed it by saying in a half-groan, "Money like that will bring in half the men in the state, and they'll be shooting at anything that moves between here and the Brazos! Tell me you didn't put an advertisement in the newspapers!"

"That's exactly what I did," Thorp said. "I ran the notice in papers in Fort Worth, Dallas, Austin, San Antonio, Galveston, and New Orleans."

Burley closed his eyes and grimaced.

"But I wrote personally to Lord Beechmuir," Thorp went

51

on. "He's the first one to arrive."

Burley looked at the Englishman. "You really think you can track down that varmint, Mr. Booth?"

"Of course I can," Booth asserted. "I tracked a particular lion halfway across the veldt once. A killer, he was, with a taste for human flesh."

"I'll take your word for it," Burley told him. "I just hope you find the Brazos Devil in a hurry, before a bunch of bounty hunters come down on this town like a plague of locusts."

Longarm figured the marshal was exaggerating a little, but probably not by much. Nothing drew folks like the chance of a big payoff. People sometimes lost all common sense when they smelled the possibility of money.

"I intend to begin my search as soon as possible," Booth assured Burley. "I'll be making my headquarters at Mr. Thorp's ranch." Booth looked over at Thorp. "I believe you said that I could use your men as beaters, Benjamin, once I've discovered the general location of the animal?"

"My hands will do whatever you say," Thorp replied with a nod. "Everything I have is at your disposal."

"Well, I'll take a small party into the bush first. Myself and Singh and a couple of men should do just fine. Then, once I've found the beast, I can send a rider back to fetch assistance."

Thorp nodded. "Sounds good to me. Why don't we go on out to the ranch so you can get settled in?" He managed to smile at Lady Beechmuir. "I'm sure her ladyship is tired after the trip up here from San Antonio."

"I wouldn't mind freshening up a bit," Helene said, returning Thorp's smile.

"It's settled then." Thorp cast a meaningful glance at Burley. "Isn't it, Mal?"

"I suppose so, Mr. Thorp," Burley responded grudgingly. "But like I said, I sure hope you find that monster in a hurry."

For Emmaline Thorp's sake, so did Longarm.

The visitors climbed back into the wagons, Booth and his wife getting into the first one along with the servant Randamar

Ghote, who handled the team. The fierce-looking Singh stepped up to the box of the second wagon and took the reins. Benjamin Thorp fetched his buggy from the nearby livery stable and led the little procession out of Cottonwood Springs.

Mal Burley watched them go and muttered under his breath, "Did you ever see anything like that?"

Longarm knew the local marshal wasn't really talking to him, but he replied anyway. "Not particularly, though I've run across a heap of strange things in my time. That big fella with the sword, I think he's what they call a Sikh. Mighty fine fighting men, from what I hear."

"I don't care. I just want the whole lot out of my town where they won't cause trouble." Burley lifted a hand and rubbed wearily at his temple. "And I wish Mr. Thorp had asked me first before posting a bounty on the Brazos Devil. I don't think he really knows what he's started."

"I don't reckon he cares," Longarm said. "He strikes me as the sort of gent who generally does what he wants."

"Yeah," Burley said, nodding slowly. "That describes Mr. Thorp, all right." He looked over at Longarm. "You're still going to stay in these parts for a few days, aren't you? Mr. Thorp seems to have forgotten that Rainey may be mixed up with his wife's disappearance, but I haven't."

Longarm thought about the developments of the morning and replied honestly, "I don't think you could get me to leave now if you wanted to, Marshal."

With the show over for the time being, Longarm went over to the Western Union office and sent that telegram to Billy Vail in Denver, informing his boss that Mitch Rainey was his prisoner and that he had been forced to kill Jimmy Lloyd in the process of apprehending the outlaws. He went on to say that Rainey was in jail in Cottonwood Springs, pending the outcome of a possible jurisdictional dispute. When the telegrapher was finished tapping out the message, he looked up from his key at Longarm and asked, "Do you want to wait for a reply, Marshal?"

"No, and don't come looking for me when one comes in either, old son," Longarm told him. "I'll come by and pick it up when I get the chance."

That ought to take care of it, he thought as he left the telegraph office and paused on the street outside to fire up a cheroot. As long as he could honestly claim that he had not received any instructions to proceed directly to Denver and jurisdictional disputes be damned, he felt justified in waiting to see what happened next in Cottonwood Springs.

He sauntered back toward the jail, and found the office empty. Longarm knew where Burley kept the ring of keys, though, so he took it from the desk and unlocked the cell-block door. Rainey looked up dispiritedly from his bunk as Longarm stepped into the aisle between the rows of cells.

"Come to badger me some more about that woman, Long?" the prisoner asked.

Longarm hooked a stool with the toe of his boot and drew it over so that he could sit down in front of Rainey's cell. "Nope," he said as he took the cheroot out of his mouth. "It just so happens that I believe your story, Rainey."

The outlaw frowned at him. "Really?"

Longarm nodded solemnly and said, "Yep."

"Well, you're the first lawdog that ever believed a word I said," Rainey allowed with a shake of his head. "Even when I was telling the truth, no man wearing a badge ever took it as gospel."

"And just how often were you really telling the truth, old son?"

A sly grin stretched across Rainey's face. "Ever' now and then."

Longarm chuckled. He didn't feel much beyond contempt for Rainey, but he could pretend otherwise if it might get him some answers. "I been thinking about that jewelry. Just where did you say you and Lloyd found it?"

"Don't recall that I ever did say exactly . . . but it was a couple miles southeast of the place where we jumped you."

Longarm nodded, thinking about what he knew of the ge-

54

ography of the area. "On the far side of the river?"

"Yeah."

That would put the spot generally opposite the point where Matt Hardcastle's savaged body had been found, Longarm decided. He said, "Was the stuff out in the open, or was it hid under a bush or something?"

"Well, there's a game trail through there, and it was at the side of the trail, not in the middle, if that's what you're asking."

Longarm considered. He knew very little about Emmaline Thorp, had no idea how coolheaded she might be in the face of danger. But it was possible she could have dropped the necklace and bracelet on purpose, hoping that the jewelry would tell any searchers she had been there. In that case she could have tossed them to the side of the trail, hoping her captor wouldn't notice. Which evidently had been what happened, or the jewelry wouldn't have been there for the two outlaws to find.

Longarm hoped his line of reasoning was correct, because that would mean Mrs. Thorp hadn't been killed outright, like Hardcastle and the Lavery boys. If whoever—or whatever—had grabbed her had had a reason for not killing her then, maybe she was still alive.

As for the existence of the creature known as the Brazos Devil, Longarm wasn't ready to make up his mind on that question just yet. Maybe Lord Beechmuir, that big-game hunter from England, would be able to find and kill the beast. Longarm recalled that gorillas had been considered legends and myths—the mysterious ape-men of Africa, they had been called—until somebody had actually captured one and brought it back to civilization. Maybe this so-called Brazos Devil was an American cousin of the gorilla.

He stood up, dropped the butt of his cheroot on the floor, and crushed it out with his boot. "I sure as hell hope you're telling the truth, Rainey," he told the prisoner. "If you're not, I don't reckon I can help you much. If Thorp finds out you

55

hurt his wife . . ." Longarm just shook his head and didn't finish the sentence.

Rainey gulped. "I said it before and I'll say it again. Jimmy and me never even saw that woman, let alone did anything to her."

Before Longarm could say anything else, he heard the front door of the office open. "Hey!" Burley exclaimed a second later when he saw the open cell-block door.

"It's all right, Marshal," Longarm called to the local lawman. "I'm just back here talking to the prisoner."

Burley appeared in the open door, a frown on his face. "I'm not sure I like the idea of you waltzing into my jail like that, Long."

Longarm shrugged. "I didn't figure you'd mind. Sorry if I stepped on your toes."

"Well, it's all right, I reckon," Burley said grudgingly. "Rainey *is* your prisoner, after all, and if I'd been here I wouldn't have minded letting you talk to him."

"Marshal, why don't you take me on to Denver, like you said you were going to?" Rainey demanded of Longarm. "I don't have anything to do with this business here."

Longarm shook his head, forestalling any protest Burley might make to the suggestion. "One bite at a time," he told Rainey. "That's the way we're going to eat *this* apple."

Burley and Longarm ate lunch together at the Red Rooster Cafe, just around the corner from the hotel. The breakfast Longarm had had in the hotel dining room had been all right, if nothing special, but the fried steak and potatoes served up at the Red Rooster made Longarm's taste buds stand up and salute. So did the peach cobbler with which he concluded the meal.

"That was mighty fine," he told Burley as they left the cafe. "Much obliged to you for recommending the place."

"The chili's even better," Burley told him, "but I wouldn't eat it if I was going to be in polite company any time in the next twenty-four hours."

Longarm grinned, then changed the subject by saying, "I was thinking about taking a ride out to Thorp's ranch. Reckon you could tell me how to find it?"

Burley had seemed almost human there for a minute—fried steak and peach cobbler had a way of doing that to a man—but his pleasant expression disappeared, only to be replaced by the usual sour frown. "What do you want to do that for?" he asked.

"Thought I'd see if he wants an extra hand along on that monster hunt he's getting up."

"I don't know if that's a good idea," Burley said dubiously.

"I can take that Englishman right to the spot where something spooked Rainey," Longarm pointed out. "Maybe he could pick up the trail there."

"Rainey claims he didn't see anything. I thought you believed his story."

"I believe he and his partner found that jewelry and didn't have anything to do with Mrs. Thorp's disappearance or Hardcastle's murder. But I know damned good and well he saw *something* that scared the piss out of him. I was there. I never saw a man so shook-up in all my life."

Burley nodded slowly. "Maybe you *should* go along with that Lord Beechmuir then. You ever have any dealings with English lords and ladies, Long?"

"A little, here and there," Longarm said. "I reckon underneath all the airs they put on, they're just folks like you and me."

"Like you, maybe." Burley shook his head. "Not like me."

He went on to give Longarm directions to Thorp's ranch, which wouldn't be difficult to find. Longarm had stabled the Appaloosa and the chestnut at the only livery barn in Cottonwood Springs, so he headed over there to saddle up the Appaloosa.

The ride out to the Rocking T took about an hour, as Longarm expected it to. He followed the Fort Griffin road west out of Cottonwood Springs and turned to the north on a smaller road before reaching the river. The ranch house was about two miles up that road.

Also as Longarm expected, the house Benjamin Thorp had built for his bride from New Orleans was quite a place. It sat on a hilltop with a spectacular view of the entire Brazos River valley to the west. There was a one-story stone house in front that might have been Thorp's original homestead and ranch house, but spreading out behind it with a wing to either side was a three-story, whitewashed frame structure with white-columned porches flanking the stone house. The arrangement gave the house a bizarre look, half Texas frontier and half antebellum plantation. Longarm found it attractive in a strange sort of way, although architecture was not one of his interests. Down the hill from the big house were barns and corrals and a long, narrow bunkhouse where the hands of the Rocking T undoubtedly lived. Longarm had seen quite a few cattle during his ride out to the ranch, and all of the animals had looked fat and healthy. Evidently, Benjamin Thorp had himself a prosperous spread here to go with that bank he owned in town.

Longarm didn't see the wagons that had brought the visitors from Cottonwood Springs. The vehicles had probably been put away in one of the barns, he thought, and the teams turned out in a corral. The trail he was following split in two, one path going toward the bunkhouse and the barns, the other curving up the hill to that hybrid house. That was the one Longarm followed.

A fence made of logs supported by stone pillars ran around the yard in front of the house. Longarm swung down from the Appaloosa and tied the reins to one of the logs. There was a gap in the fence that served as a gate, with a flagstone walk on the other side of it. Longarm followed that to the front door of the stone structure. He slapped a heavy brass knocker up and down a couple of times.

To his surprise, the big Sikh answered the summons. Longarm was just about as tall as Absalom Singh. He nodded to the fierce-looking foreigner and said, "I've come to see Mr.

58

Thorp and Lord Beechmuir. Name's Custis Long. I'm a U.S. deputy marshal.''

Longarm didn't know if Singh spoke any English or not. Stolid and expressionless, the man stepped back to let Longarm enter the house.

Benjamin Thorp came through a door on the other side of the room, which was furnished with a heavy sofa, a couple of chairs, and a bearskin rug on the puncheon floor. On one side of the room was a fireplace with a massive stone mantel over it. A pair of horns decorated the wall above the fireplace. Longarm could tell from the wide sweep of the horns that they had come from a Texas longhorn.

Thorp had a big cigar in his mouth. He took it out and said, "What are you doing here, Marshal?"

"Came to talk to you and Lord Beechmuir. I want to go along on the hunt for that critter."

"I thought you didn't believe in the Brazos Devil," Thorp said, lifting one eyebrow in an expression of smug surprise.

"I'm not sure I do," Longarm said honestly, "but I'm willing to keep an open mind about it."

Thorp sighed, and suddenly he looked older again. "I find that I *have* to believe in the creature, Marshal Long. As horrible as being taken captive by it might be for Emmaline, I think she has a better chance of still being alive if that's what happened. If that outlaw Rainey is lying . . . if Emmaline wound up in the hands of him and his partner . . . then I have no doubt she's dead now."

"Chances are you're right," Longarm agreed, being brutally frank about it. "I reckon for your sake—and the sake of your wife—I hope there really is a Brazos Devil too."

Thorp inclined his head toward the door behind him. "Well, come on in. I don't believe you met Lord and Lady Beechmuir in town. I'll introduce you."

Longarm followed Thorp into the other part of the house, into a much more tastefully appointed drawing room. The influence of Emmaline Thorp was readily visible here in the rugs, the delicate furniture, the crystal chandelier, and the lace

59

curtains over the windows. This could have been a drawing room in a Southern mansion. John and Helene Booth were seated on a small divan, both of them holding glasses of brandy. The Indian servant, Ghote, hovered in the background.

Booth came to his feet as Longarm and Thorp entered the room. The rancher said, "Lord Beechmuir, I neglected to introduce this gentleman while we were in town. This is Marshal Custis Long, who also has an interest in this affair. He has a prisoner in jail in Cottonwood Springs who is involved, at least indirectly, in my wife's disappearance."

Booth extended a hand. "It's a great pleasure to meet you, Marshal. However, I was under the impression that Mr. Burley was the local constable."

"He is," Longarm said as he returned the Englishman's firm grip. "I'm a deputy United States marshal."

"Ah, a representative of your country's government," said Booth. "I'm pleased and honored to make your acquaintance." He turned and held out a hand toward his wife. "Allow me to present Lady Beechmuir."

Longarm smiled at Helene and acted on an impulse, bending over the hand she held up to him and brushing his lips across the back as he took it. "The honor's all mine, ma'am."

"My, aren't you the charming gentleman, even if you do look like a cowboy, Marshal Long," she said.

"I prefer to think of myself as a diamond in the rough, ma'am."

The fires he had seen in her eyes earlier were banked now, but he could still feel some heat coming from her. Not being in the habit of standing around and flirting with married women—at least not while their husbands were in the room—Longarm released her hand and smiled politely at her, then turned back to Thorp and Lord Beechmuir.

"Like I told Mr. Thorp," he said to the Englishman, "I rode out here to volunteer to go along with you when you start looking for the Brazos Devil."

"Do you have any big-game hunting experience, Marshal Long?"

"Well, I've shot my share of grizzly bears and mountain lions," Longarm said, "but only when they were fixing to jump me. I've had more experience hunting men, and those who have seen it say the Brazos Devil is half-man."

"And half-monster," Thorp put in. "But we'll be glad for the help, won't we, Lord Beechmuir?"

"Of course. Always good to have another competent chap along for a hunt."

Helene said, "Marshal Long looks very competent indeed."

Longarm figured he had better ignore that, but then chivalry got the better of him and he nodded to her. "Thank you, ma'am." To Thorp he said, "What time do you plan on leaving in the morning?"

"We'll be on the trail early. You think you can show us where Rainey saw whatever he claims he *didn't* see?"

"That's just what I planned to do," Longarm said.

Booth raised his glass of brandy. "I propose a toast, gentlemen . . . although perhaps that's not the proper thing to do, considering the plight that has brought us here, Benjamin."

Thorp shook his head and said, "No, that's all right, your lordship. I'm very concerned about my wife's safety, of course, but I realize this is an important undertaking for you too. Hunting down a creature like the one we've got around here will make you more famous than ever."

"Yes, but your dear bride's return is of course the most important thing."

While Thorp and Booth were trading those comments, the servant Ghote glided forward and pressed a glass of brandy into Longarm's hand. Longarm noticed that Ghote had a fresh glass for Lady Beechmuir as well. Her ladyship had polished off the first one.

Booth raised his glass. "To the Brazos Devil, my friends," he said in his mellifluous voice. "And to us, the men who will bring the creature back . . . dead or alive."

Chapter 7

Thorp insisted that Longarm stay for supper. The man was distracted by the situation and his worry about his wife, but the Western tradition of hospitality ran deep. Longarm accepted the invitation, and was glad he did. The middle-aged black woman who served as cook and housekeeper for the Rocking T dished up some fine grub, Longarm discovered as he put away several helpings of ham, sweet potatoes, and greens.

After the meal, Longarm, Thorp, and Lord Beechmuir went into the main room of the stone house, which Longarm figured served as a study of sorts for the rancher. As he handed cigars to the other two men, Thorp confirmed that this part of the house had been his original dwelling when he'd started the Rocking T, long before he went to New Orleans on a business trip and unexpectedly brought back a bride.

Smoking cigars and having another brandy with Thorp and Booth was enjoyable enough, but Longarm didn't want to linger too long. "I'd best be heading back to town so I can get some sleep," he said after a few minutes. "I'll be out here around sunup in the morning, Mr. Thorp."

"That'll be fine, Marshal," Thorp said with a nod. "Is there anything you'll need?"

"Well, if you've got a good Winchester I could borrow, I'm without a saddle gun. That rented nag of mine ran off with mine when he spooked yesterday. I was hoping he might wander into Cottonwood Springs so I could get my rig back, but that doesn't look like it's going to happen."

"I've got plenty of spare rifles, and you're welcome to use one of them."

"Better yet," Lord Beechmuir said, "I'd be delighted to have you use one of my guns, Marshal Long. Have you ever fired a Markham & Halliday elephant gun?"

"No, sir, can't say as I have," Longarm replied dryly.

"Quite a magnificent weapon, don't you know! If you need to drop a charging rogue elephant in its tracks, you couldn't want a better gun."

Longarm coughed discreetly. "I appreciate the offer, your lordship, but I reckon that'd be a mite too much power for me to handle. I'll stick with a Winchester '73."

"Certainly. A man should be comfortable with his weapons, I always say."

Longarm looked around for his hat, not quite sure where he had put it, but Ghote was suddenly there, holding out the Stetson to him. Longarm took it from the servant, who seemed to move about as quietly as a Comanche in the dark of the moon. He settled the hat on his head, nodded to Thorp and Booth, and said, "I'll see you gents in the morning. Say good night to Lady Beechmuir for me."

"Indeed I shall," Booth assured him.

Earlier in the day, Thorp had had Longarm's Appaloosa taken down to the barns, unsaddled, rubbed down, and grained and watered. Longarm headed down the hill now, figuring he could find one of the ranch hands around the barns who could tell him where to locate the horse. He was only halfway down the hill, however, making his way past a grove of oaks, when a soft voice stopped him.

"Good evening, Marshal Long," Helene Booth said from

63

the shadows underneath the trees.

Longarm stopped and turned toward the oaks. Instinctively he reached up and gave the brim of his hat a polite tug. "Evenin', ma'am," he said. "Pardon my asking, but what might you be doing out here in the dark?"

"Getting a breath of air." He saw movement in the shadows as she came closer to him. "It's a lovely night, don't you think?"

"Yes, ma'am," Longarm said.

And it was. The air was crisp with autumn coolness and clear enough so that every star overhead seemed to sparkle individually.

"Would you be kind enough to stroll with me for a moment?" asked Helene.

"Well, ma'am, I'm sure your husband would be glad to take a walk with you. I just left him up at the house."

Longarm was taking a step back toward the house as he spoke, but Lady Beechmuir stopped him by saying, "I've just spent several interminable days cramped up in a wagon with my husband, Marshal Long. I've had an abundance of his company, thank you very much."

"I was just on my way to get my horse and head back to town," he said.

"Surely you can spare me a few minutes, Custis. Do your friends call you that? I shall call you Custis."

She didn't sound like she would tolerate any argument on the subject, so he just nodded and said, "That'd be fine, ma'am."

"And you simply *must* stop calling me ma'am!"

"All right . . . your ladyship."

She made a noise of exasperation. "We're not in England now, Custis. My name is Helene. Call me whatever you would call any other frontier woman in these circumstances."

"Well, I'd likely call her missus," said Longarm.

Helene laughed and stepped even closer to him. She was on the edge of the shadows now, and he could see her much better. He could smell her too, a heady mixture of the brandy

64

on her breath, the perfume she wore, and an undeniable undercurrent of woman-scent. Just taking a deep breath around her, Longarm thought, was enough to get a man all hot and bothered.

"Call me Helene," she said, and again her tone brooked no argument. "Please, take my hand and walk with me." She held out her hand toward him.

He might get away from here quicker and easier if he just played along with her for a spell, Longarm figured. Besides, he hardly ever ran the other way when a beautiful woman wanted to flirt with him, even one who was married, although he did try to steer clear of causing serious trouble between a husband and wife. He reached out and took her hand. What could she do? he asked himself. Try to seduce him right here within sight of the house where she and her husband were staying? Didn't seem likely.

Which only went to show how wrong a gent could be sometimes, he realized a moment after he had stepped into the gloom underneath the trees with Lady Beechmuir. She had her mouth pressed hotly to his and was rubbing those noble curves all over him.

Longarm was taken by surprise, so when she practically lunged against him, it was natural enough that his arms went around her. And when her hot, wet tongue speared between his lips to invade his mouth and fence with his own tongue, it was only to be expected that his shaft would spring to attention and prod its hard length against her soft flesh. She ground her belly against him, moaning low in her throat as she felt the size of him through his trousers and her gown.

Longarm managed to get his mouth away from hers long enough to say breathlessly, "Hold on there!"

Her hand came up and boldly caressed his groin as she laughed and said, "Hold on where? Here?"

Longarm gritted his teeth together and tried to tell both his brain and his body that this wasn't a good idea. The way Helene was toying with him, he wasn't going to be able to think of anything in a minute. He reached down, took hold of her wrist, and moved it away, despite the fact that it was a difficult thing for him to do. It took a great deal of willpower.

"Now look here, ma'am—"

"Helene! You said you'd call me Helene."

"Ma'am," he insisted, "you're a married woman. If that ain't enough, your husband is right up the hill there, and he's an English lord at that."

"You're not telling me anything I don't already know, Custis," she said as she tried to grope him again and he fended her off. "What's your point—no, wait, I think I've found it."

Longarm cussed under his breath and disengaged her hand again as firmly as he could without hurting her. "I'm no prude," he told her, "and I reckon I've had a few married ladies in my bed at one time or another, but this just ain't right. You'd better let me go on back to Cottonwood Springs whilst you go back to your husband, ma'am."

Abruptly, she pulled loose from his grip and moved away a step. "You are a most exasperating man!" she exclaimed. "Don't you find me attractive?"

"I sure do," he replied honestly, "but that's got nothing to do with it."

Helene laughed again, and the sound was full of scorn. "My God," she said. "John comes here hunting for some mythical beast, and I find something I thought was equally fanciful: a moral man."

"Most folks wouldn't call me that," Longarm said, also honestly.

"Yes, but they'd be wrong. They just don't know you well enough. Tell me, Custis, what would you be doing right if I *wasn't* married?"

Longarm took a deep breath. "Well, ma'am, I reckon I'd have that pretty gown of yours up around your hips and we'd be getting a whole heap better acquainted, if you get my drift."

She laughed again, but this time she sounded genuinely amused. "Indeed I do get your drift, Marshal Long." She sighed. "But I fear that's all I'll be getting from you tonight."

66

"Yes, ma'am, I expect that's true."

"All right. Go on back to Cottonwood Springs. I know when I'm wasting my time." Helene hesitated, then added, "But I warn you, Custis . . . I regard you now as a challenge. And I have always *adored* challenges."

Longarm didn't like the sound of that at all, but there wasn't much he could do about it. He tugged on the brim of his hat one more time and backed quickly out of the trees. "Good night, ma'am."

"Good night, Marshal."

He started walking toward the barns again, puffing out his cheeks and then blowing out the air in a sigh of relief as he went. That had been a close call. Chances were, nothing would have happened if he had gone ahead and given Lady Beechmuir what she wanted.

But he was damned if he wanted to go monster-hunting the next morning with a man he had cuckolded the night before. Especially since Lord Beechmuir would probably be carrying one of those big old elephant guns . . .

Something made Longarm pause suddenly and look over his shoulder. He thought he caught a glimpse of movement on the hill between the trees and the house. It might have been Helene going back in, he thought.

Or it might have been something else, and he wondered where that slippery-footed servant Ghote was right about now. Could the fellow have been spying on his mistress and seen and overheard what had happened in the grove? Longarm didn't much like that thought, but there was nothing he could do about it now.

He walked on quickly toward the barn, anxious to put the Rocking T behind him for the time being.

Longarm had told Benjamin Thorp that he wanted to get some sleep, but he wasn't really tired enough to go up to his hotel room when he got back to Cottonwood Springs. The sound of piano music floating past the batwing doors of the town's only good-sized saloon drew his attention, and Longarm realized that what he really wanted was a drink of good rye whiskey and maybe a hand or two of cards in a friendly poker game. That would relax him enough so he could get a good night's sleep. He angled the Appaloosa toward the saloon, which was just up the block from the hotel.

The only trouble with his plan was that all hell broke loose before he got where he was going.

A scream suddenly overrode the strains of the piano, and a man hurtled out through the batwings to sprawl limply in the street in front of Longarm. There was a sound like a mountain lion's howl inside the saloon, and it took Longarm a second to realize that the awful screech had come from the throat of a human being. Shouted curses and more screams filled the air, followed by the crashing of furniture and the unmistakable thud of fists against flesh.

Longarm reined in the horse and thought for a moment about turning around and going back to the hotel. He had seen probably a hundred saloon brawls in his time, and had participated in too damned many of them. With any luck, Mal Burley would be along pretty soon to break this one up before it got too serious.

But then a gun went off a couple of times inside the saloon and the screaming got worse. Longarm bit back a curse and sent the Appaloosa forward again. He had carried a badge for too blasted long to start turning his back on trouble now.

Longarm had heard only two shots, but there was no telling if that was a good sign or not. He swung down from the saddle, paused just long enough to loop the Appaloosa's reins around the hitch rack alongside a dozen other horses, then stepped up onto the saloon's porch with one stride of his long legs. His right hand reached across his body to make sure his Colt was loose in its holster before he slapped the batwings aside and stepped into the melee.

The first thing Longarm saw was a chair flying through the air at his head. He ducked frantically. The chair missed him and smashed into the batwings behind him, tearing one of the swinging doors loose from its hinges. Longarm heard that hideous howl again, and then a deep voice bellowed out over the confusion, "I'm Catamount Jack, and I'm a ring-tailed wonder!" The man the voice belonged to threw back his head and howled again.

Longarm could see that because the man stood taller than any of the knot of struggling figures around him. As Longarm watched, the man who called himself Catamount Jack reached out, snagged two of the combatants by the shoulders, and rammed their skulls together with enough force to knock out both of them. They slumped to the floor when the big man let go of them. At the same time, Catamount Jack was shrugging off the blows that rained in on him as if he didn't even feel them.

He wore buckskins and a broad-brimmed, nearly shapeless brown hat. He was thin, appearing almost gaunt because of his height, but when his knobby fists snapped out into the faces of his opponents, there was plenty of power behind the punches. The blows sent men staggering backward or falling on their rumps when they landed.

Longarm saw a man in the silk shirt, fancy vest, and cutaway coat of a professional gambler waving a pistol around. "Get out of the way!" the man shouted at the crowd around Catamount Jack. "I'll plug the old bastard!"

Longarm figured the gambler was the one who had fired the other two shots. The man was already impatiently easing back the hammer for another try. Longarm moved fast, reaching over the gambler's shoulder with his left hand. His fingers closed around the cylinder of the pistol, preventing it from turning.

"Let go, you son of a bitch!" the gambler yelled as he twisted toward Longarm. Longarm hit him then, a short punch that traveled no more than six inches but still possessed enough power to jerk the gambler's head to the side. The man's eyes rolled up in their sockets and he unhinged at the knees. Longarm plucked the gun easily from his grip as he fell.

After easing down the hammer, Longarm stuck the pistol

behind his belt and turned his attention once more to the fracas in the center of the room. There was no way of knowing what had started the battle, but evidently it was everybody else in the room versus Catamount Jack. Jack's mallet-like fists had already laid out more than half a dozen of his opponents, but he was still outnumbered more than twenty to one.

Make that twenty to *two,* Longarm thought as he saw a man swinging a whiskey bottle at the back of Catamount Jack's head, only to have a smaller figure in buckskins dart out of nowhere, kick him in the groin, then clout him over the head with a six-gun when he bent over in agony. Catamount Jack had at least one ally.

Or maybe two, Longarm grudgingly admitted, because no matter what the provocation, no matter who had started it, he didn't like to see a fight this uneven. Even as he hoped he wasn't making a mistake, he reached out, grabbed the shoulder of one of the men attacking Catamount Jack, and spun the gent around. Longarm slammed a fist into the middle of the man's surprised face.

He was able to down two more of the brawlers before they realized what was happening. Then some of them turned away from Catamount Jack to deal with this new threat. Longarm buried his fist in the belly of one man and shoved him aside to backhand another. He was starting to absorb some punishment himself now, as some of the flurry of punches got past his guard and rocked him back a step. Somebody grabbed him from the side, and he drove an elbow into the man's solar plexus. Another man got hold of his coat collar and jerked him off balance.

Longarm knew he couldn't afford to fall down. Once you were on the floor, it was too easy to get trampled in a melee like this. He had seen men killed that way, stomped to death by other men who didn't know or care who they were stepping on. He slapped one of his booted feet on the floor to steady himself, spreading his legs wide apart. He couldn't see Catamount Jack anymore; the press of angry men around him was too thick.

Suddenly some of them fell back, and Longarm caught a glimpse of that smaller, buckskin-clad figure. The man had holstered his pistol and was wielding a broken chair leg now, lashing out around him and dropping his larger opponents left and right. Longarm grinned, grateful for the respite, and punched a gent in the jaw. The figure in buckskins jabbed another man in the belly, then slapped the makeshift club against the side of his head, dropping him. Longarm grabbed one of his opponents, head-butted him, then shoved him into two more men. Their feet and legs got tangled up and all three of them went crashing down. Longarm found himself bumping shoulders with the figure in buckskins.

"Pretty good fight, eh?" Longarm grunted as he blocked a blow and lashed out with a punch of his own.

"Damn right!" came the reply in a voice full of excitement. A woman's voice.

Longarm's head snapped around, his eyes widening in surprise, and he found himself staring into blue eyes above a nice little nose that had a scattering of freckles across it. Blond curls were escaping from underneath the hat the woman in buckskins had crammed down on his—her!—head. Longarm opened his mouth to say something else.

Then something cracked across the back of his head before he could speak, and felt himself tumbling forward. A boot dug into his ribs in a vicious kick as he fell. He heard the woman in buckskins yell, "Hey!" Then she cried out in pain.

Longarm's shoulder hit the floor first. He rolled over, coming to rest on his back just as a weight landed on top of him, knocking all the air out of his lungs. As consciousness slipped away from him, he realized that for the second time tonight, he had his arms full of firm female flesh.

And if a fella had to get himself knocked out, he supposed, that was as good a way to plummet into blackness as any, and better than most.

71

Chapter 8

"By all rights, I ought to lock you up back there with the others," Mal Burley was saying angrily half an hour later. "The only reason I didn't is because you're a fellow lawman and I thought I ought to give you the benefit of the doubt. You *were* trying to break up that fight, weren't you, Marshal Long? The witnesses I talked to said you were right in the middle of it."

Longarm took the wet towel off the back of his neck and sighed. "I appreciate the professional courtesy, Marshal," he said wearily. "To tell the truth, I'm not sure now what I was doing, but it seemed like a good idea at the time."

Burley snorted. "Well, I know who started the fight at least. That hombre who calls himself Catamount Jack seems damned proud of the fact that he did. He hasn't stopped talking about it since I threw him and that wildcat daughter of his into a cell."

Longarm lifted his head and said, "You locked up the girl?"

"She was part of the fight too," Burley said defensively. "I heard eyewitness accounts of how she knocked out at least three men. She may have even cracked Jordy Higgins' skull!"

72

Longarm stood up. His head still hurt, but not as bad as it had when he first woke up on the cot in the jail's back room where Burley sometimes slept. The marshal of Cottonwood Springs had been standing over him, glaring down at him, and Burley had lost no time in informing Longarm of what had happened. Longarm had been out cold on the floor of the saloon when Burley came in with a shotgun and broke up the brawl by firing one of the weapon's barrels into the ceiling. Commandeering some "volunteers" from the crowd, Burley had ordered that all the unconscious combatants be dragged down to the jail, while he had used the shotgun to prod the ones who were still upright into moving. The cell block was full at the moment, and Doc Carson was in there now checking over the men who had been knocked out. The physician had already examined Longarm and proclaimed him to be all right, with the exception of a bad headache from the blow he had suffered.

Moving on legs that were still a little shaky, Longarm headed toward the cell-block door. "Is the girl all right?" he asked. "You said she's Catamount Jack's daughter?"

"That's what she claims," replied Burley, "and I don't know why anybody would say that unless it was true! She wasn't knocked out like you, just stunned a mite. Doc's already checked her out and said she'll be just fine."

Longarm swung open the door, which was closed but not locked. There were six cells back here, three on each side of the wide aisle. Mitch Rainey was in the first cell on the right, Catamount Jack and his daughter were in the second one, and the rest of the brawlers from the saloon were crowded into the remaining four cells. There was a lot of groaning and cussing going on among them.

There were no complaints coming from the cell containing Catamount Jack and the girl, however. They were sitting side by side on the bunk, arms around each other's shoulders, bellowing out the obscene lyrics of an old sailor's song. Longarm frowned at them, and even Rainey, in the next cell, was looking a little askance at the pair.

The girl stopped singing when she saw Longarm. "There he is!" she called out. "There's that handsome fella I told you about, Pa."

She had taken off her hat so that her honey-colored curls spilled around her shoulders. Her face was smudged with dirt and had a smear of blood on the forehead, but she was still a reasonably attractive young woman. She grinned at Longarm.

Catamount Jack stood up and came over to the door of the cell. He thrust his ham-like right hand through the bars. "Hear tell you pitched in on our side durin' that little fracas, stranger," he said. "Much obliged, even though me an' Lucy didn't really need no help. We'd've cleaned up that bunch sooner or later."

Longarm shook hands with the man, expecting a bone-crushing grip and getting one.

"I'm Catamount Jack Vermilion," the big man went on, "and this here's my girl-child Lucy. Who might you be?"

"Custis Long." Longarm paused, then added, "I'm a deputy United States marshal."

Catamount Jack's eyes narrowed. "Lawman, eh? First time one o' them critters ever tried to give me a hand. But like I said, I'm obliged anyway."

"What in blazes was that brawl all about?" asked Longarm.

Catamount Jack jerked a callused thumb over his shoulder. "Some no-good scoundrels made aspersions about my little girl's honor. Said no self-respectin' female'd come into a saloon wearin' buckskins. Natcherly, we had to set 'em straight, and their pards took offense at the way we done it."

"You damn near busted their heads open," Burley said from behind Longarm.

Catamount Jack leaned over to peer around Longarm and frown at Burley. "Ain't nobody insults my little girl without payin' for it!"

Longarm turned to look at the local badge. "Did those witnesses you were talking about say whether or not the fight started the way Mr. Vermilion says it did?"

"Well," Burley said grudgingly, "I reckon there could

74

have been some comments made about the young lady before the trouble started. But that didn't give them the right to try to tear up the whole saloon!''

"We can settle this right easy," Catamount Jack proposed. "How much did the damages come to? I don't mind payin' for 'em. Hell, ever' good fight's got its price.''

"I talked to Dave Kilroy, the owner of the saloon," Burley said. "He put the damages at two hundred dollars.''

That figure sounded a bit inflated to Longarm, but he didn't say anything. It wouldn't matter anyway. From the looks of the ragged buckskins worn by Catamount Jack and Lucy, they likely didn't have two dollars between them, let alone two hundred.

What Catamount Jack did next surprised both Longarm and Burley. The big man reached inside his shirt and pulled out a leather pouch. The clinking sound of coins came from the pouch as he opened the drawstring top. "Fair enough, I reckon," said Catamount Jack as he spilled double eagles into the open palm of his other hand. He counted out ten of the twenty-dollar gold pieces and put the others back in the pouch, then extended his hand through the bars with the two hundred dollars. "There you go.''

Burley didn't take the coins. "Where'd you get loot like that?" he asked suspiciously. "I don't recall hearing about any bank robberies around here lately.''

"Bank robberies!" Catamount Jack repeated, sounding offended. "Hell, that's honest-earned money, Marshal. Lucy and me been wolvin' all summer up Montana way. The cattlemen up there still pay good money to get rid o' wolves.''

"All right," Burley said with a sigh. He took the double eagles from Catamount Jack. "There's still the matter of the fine for disturbing the peace.''

Longarm inclined his head toward the men in the other cells. "Are you planning to fine all of those gents too, Marshal? Seems to me they were disturbing the peace just as much as Mr. Vermilion and his daughter.''

"Yeah!" Lucy suddenly said. "There wouldn't've been no

75

fight if they hadn't cast 'spersions on me.''

Burley stood there for a moment, a frown on his forehead and a grimace pulling at his mouth. "All right, I'll drop the charges against everybody," he said. "I suppose you want me to let you out of there now."

"Well," Catamount Jack said, his tone surprisingly mild, "I *did* pay for the damages we done. . . . "

Burley took the ring of keys from his belt and opened the cell door, still making a face. Catamount Jack turned and held out a hand to his daughter. Lucy picked up her hat, jammed it back on her head, and stood up to join him. Longarm stepped back so both of them could leave the cell.

Catamount Jack slapped a big hand on his back, almost staggering him. "How 'bout havin' a drink with us, Custis?" he asked. "I reckon you're the closest thing we got to a friend in this town tonight."

Longarm started to decline the offer, then decided that it might be wise to keep an eye on the two of them for a while, just to make sure they didn't start any more fights. Besides, if Lucy Vermilion was cleaned up a mite, he had a feeling she would be a damned nice-looking woman.

"Sure," he said with a nod. "I'll have a drink with you."

"I don't want any more trouble," warned Burley.

"There won't be," Longarm promised him.

Some of the other prisoners, who had heard everything that was said, began yelling to be released from their cells since they weren't going to be charged with anything. Burley jerked a thumb at the cell-block door and said to Longarm, "Get 'em out of here before I let any of these other jaspers loose."

"Good idea," Longarm agreed. He steered Catamount Jack and Lucy toward the door.

Once they were outside, Catamount Jack took a deep breath and slapped his hands against his chest. "Air always smells better when you're a free man," he declared.

Longarm understood and agreed with that sentiment. He said dryly, "That's why I try to stay out of jail."

"That ain't fair," Lucy protested. "It ain't our fault we got locked up—"

"Yes, it was, girl," her father broke in. "Might as well be honest about it, since Custis here is our friend. We was both in a mood to howl tonight, Custis, and if them cowboys hadn't said what they did, likely we'd've found some other reason to start a ruckus. Ain't that right, Lucy?"

"Well, maybe," she admitted, then changed the subject by saying, "I thought we were goin' to have another drink."

"There's only the one saloon in town," Longarm said, "and I'm not sure any of us would be too welcome in there again tonight. But maybe I could duck in and buy a bottle without getting the proprietor too upset. Maryland rye all right with you folks?"

"Hell of a lot better'n the panther piss we usually drink!" Catamount Jack said with a laugh. He took out his money pouch and handed Longarm one of the double eagles. "That'll be fine, Custis. Whilst you're doin' that, we'll get our mules. They're tied up at the rack in front of the saloon."

Quite a few bottles of liquor had gotten smashed during the brawl, but luck was with Longarm. There was an unbroken bottle of rye behind the bar, and Dave Kilroy was glad to sell it to him, especially once Longarm had informed the saloonkeeper that Marshal Burley had collected enough money from Catamount Jack to pay for the damages.

"I hope that wild man never comes in here again," Kilroy said with a shudder. "I've seen my share of loco customers, but he was just about the worst." Kilroy glared across the bar at Longarm. "And you just about broke the jaw of my best dealer, I'm told."

"Mighty sorry about that," Longarm said contritely. "Seemed like the best thing to do at the time, considering how he was waving that gun around. I figured if I didn't stop him, somebody innocent might get shot."

"Nobody innocent ever comes in a saloon," Kilroy said, then shrugged. "But I reckon you're right. Still, I don't want Vermilion and his girl in here again."

"I'll make sure they know to steer clear of your place," Longarm promised.

He carried the bottle of rye outside and found Catamount Jack and Lucy waiting in the middle of the street. They were leading four mules. Two of the beasts wore saddles, while the others were pack animals.

"Where did you plan to spend the night?" Longarm asked as he gave Catamount Jack the change from the twenty-dollar gold piece. "I think there are some vacant rooms at the hotel."

The big man snorted in disgust. "Hotel?" he repeated. "I don't mind buyin' a bottle of booze or payin' for the damages from a good fight, but I ain't throwin' away good money on no hotel room. Not as long as there's ground for a bed and a starry sky for the ceilin'."

"We figured we'd camp just outside of town," Lucy said. "Got a good place picked out and everything."

"All right," Longarm said. "Lead the way."

As he walked to the western outskirts of Cottonwood Springs with Catamount Jack and Lucy, he realized the evening certainly hadn't turned out the way he'd thought it would when he returned from Thorp's Rocking T ranch. For one thing, he still had a headache from being clouted. And he sure as hell hadn't expected to run into two such colorful characters. But he found himself liking the Vermilions, father and daughter, and once he had shared some of the rye with them, maybe they would settle down for the night and he could return to the hotel knowing there wouldn't be any more trouble.

A thought occurred to Longarm as they left the lights of the settlement behind. "Might not be a very good idea to camp out here after all," he said. "There's some sort of wild critter that may be running loose around here. Several people have been killed so far. I don't know if it would come this close to town, but you might not want to take the chance."

Catamount Jack laughed and patted the stock of a rifle sticking up from the saddle boot on his mule. "This here's a Sharps Big Fifty I used to kill more'n five thousand buffalo in my time, Custis. You know how much kick this carbine's got?"

"Plenty," Longarm admitted.

"As long as I got this Big Fifty with me, I ain't scared of no critter, man or beast. And if you're talkin' about the Brazos Devil, I *hope* he shows up! That'd suit me just fine."

"You know about the Brazos Devil?" Longarm asked with a surprised frown.

"Know about him? Hell, that varmint's the reason we're here, ain't it, Lucy?"

"That's right," Lucy said. "We're goin' to get us that twenty-thousand-dollar bounty when we bring in the Brazos Devil's head!"

Mal Burley sighed wearily as he sank down in the chair behind his desk. He put his boots on the little wooden footstool he kept in the desk's kneehole; otherwise his feet wouldn't reach the floor, and as somebody who had been short all his life, he knew how tiresome that was.

Even more tiresome were all the complaints he had heard as he unlocked the cell doors and let the prisoners file out of the jail. It wasn't enough that he wasn't charging them with disturbing the peace. They were mad because he hadn't fined Catamount Jack Vermilion either. The way they saw it, Catamount Jack had started the whole thing, so he ought to have to pay.

"Just be glad I didn't make you pass the hat to cover the damages to Kilroy's place," Burley had snapped at them. "Vermilion paid the whole thing, and you boys aren't out a red cent!"

That had shut them up for the most part, although there had been some grumbling still going on as they left. Nobody was locked up back in the cell block now except Mitch Rainey, and Burley was glad of that. He despised the outlaw, and believed there was a better than even chance Rainey had had something to do with Emmaline Thorp's disappearance and Matt Hardcastle's murder. But Burley had to admit Rainey hadn't caused any trouble during the more than twenty-four hours he had been locked up here.

Burley took off his hat and tossed it on the desk. He closed his eyes and scrubbed a hand over his face, then gave a little shake of his head. He reached for the desk drawer where he kept a small silver flask. One nip and he'd be ready to head for his cot.

That was when the prisoner started screaming bloody murder.

Actually the cries were just incoherent screeches, Burley realized as he leaped to his feet and ran toward the cell-block door. As he fumbled the key into the lock and turned it, he heard Rainey begin to say frantically, "Get it away from me, get it away from me!"

Could be Rainey was just having a fit, Burley thought, but he had to be certain. He pulled his gun from its holster as he swung the door open and ran into the cell block.

Rainey was squirming around on the bunk, kicking his feet and slapping his hands at empty air. "Get it away, get it away!" he screamed again.

"What is it?" yelled Burley. "I don't see anything!"

"At the window!" Rainey shrieked. "At the window! It's in the alley! God, don't let it get me!"

Burley thought Rainey was imagining things, but then he heard a rustling noise and a growl coming from outside the small, barred window in the cell. The marshal's breath caught in his throat. The way Rainey was acting, the Brazos Devil could be right outside the jail!

Burley's heart began pounding wildly in his chest. He wasn't sure why the Brazos Devil would risk coming all the way into town like this, but if he could capture or kill the beast, he could collect that twenty-thousand-dollar bounty from Benjamin Thorp. Not only that, it would improve his shaky standing with the town's most influential citizen. Those thoughts flashed through Burley's head in an instant, and the next second he was unlocking the door of the cell. He rushed across to the window, ready to stick his gun out through the bars and start blasting.

He lifted himself on his toes, straining to peer through the opening. Unable to quite see out, Burley grabbed the slops bucket from underneath the bunk and overturned it, heedless of the foul mess that it made on the floor. Rainey was still cowering on the bunk, eyes wide with terror as he made feeble pushing motions with his hands. Burley placed the overturned bucket under the window and stepped up on it, balancing himself as he looked out.

There wasn't much light in the alley alongside the jail, but enough illumination filtered into it from the moon and stars that Burley would be able to see anything as big as the Brazos Devil. He twisted his neck from side to side, searching anxiously for any sign of the creature. He heard the growling sound again, and it made the hair on the back of his neck stand up.

Then, right underneath the window, a dog barked.

"Hey!" Burley exclaimed. "There's nothing out here but an old mutt—"

He was turning as he spoke, directing the angry words at Rainey. Before he could finish the sentence, however, Rainey's shoulder slammed into his midsection, smashing him back against the wall. Burley grunted in pain and tried to bring his gun around, the bitter realization that he had been tricked flooding through him. Rainey grabbed his wrist before Burley could bring the weapon into play, and used his other hand to hook a vicious punch into Burley's midsection. Burley felt himself falling off the overturned bucket.

Rainey caught the marshal around the throat and drove his head against the wall again. Burley went limp, the gun slipping from his fingers. Blackness closed in around him, and his last thought before he passed out was a curse at what a fool he had been.

Chapter 9

The spot Catamount Jack and Lucy had picked for their campsite was a clearing in a grove of cottonwoods northwest of
town. A small spring-fed creek ran through the trees, and
Longarm supposed that was where the settlement had gotten
its name. He had to admit the clearing was a pretty place to
camp. An evening breeze, cool but not cold, was blowing
through the partially bare branches of the cottonwoods, making a lulling sound. The grass on the ground was still thick
from the previous summer. Catamount Jack and Lucy unsaddled their riding mules and unloaded the pack animals while
Longarm got a small fire going. When the mules had been
staked out for the night, the three people settled down beside
the flickering flames and began passing around the bottle of
rye. Then Longarm was finally able to satisfy his curiosity.

"How in blazes did you find out about the Brazos Devil
and the bounty Thorp put on it?" he asked. "I thought you
said the two of you had been up in Montana all summer."

"We were," Catamount Jack replied. "But ever' fall we
come down here and pay a visit to my sister over in Austin.
She's a widow lady, you know, and don't have no fam'ly but
us."

"And you saw the notice Thorp put in the Austin paper," Longarm guessed.

"Actually, I did," Lucy said. "Pa ain't much of a hand for readin', but he made sure I knew how. I can even cipher a mite."

Catamount Jack lifted the bottle to his lips and took a long swig. Then, after wiping the back of his hand across his mouth, he handed the rye to Longarm and said, "When I was naught but a boy, back in the last days of the Shinin' Times, I knew men who couldn't read a word—but they could recite whole chunks of the Bible and practic'ly ever' word that Shakespeare fella ever wrote. When those old boys went to spoutin' passages, though, I always wondered . . . how did I know they was gettin' it right? I swore then that if I ever had any young'uns, I'd see to it that they could read the words for theirselves, rather than havin' to listen to somebody else recite 'em." He smiled fondly at the young woman. "Well, Lucy's the onliest child I was ever blessed with, seein' as how her mama died when Lucy was just a bitty little babe, but I always done the best by her I knew how. She can read an' do her numbers, like she said, and she can run all day like an Apache, shoot better'n nine out o' ten men, drink most fellas under the table, and rassle an alligator singlehanded. Yes, sir, I'm mighty proud of her."

"Hush, Pa," Lucy said, and Longarm thought she was actually blushing—or maybe it was just the firelight that made her look that way. "You're borin' poor Custis to death."

"No, that's fine," Longarm said. He took a little nip from the bottle. "A father's got a right to be proud of his daughter." He grinned and handed the bottle back to Catamount Jack.

The level of rye in the bottle dropped considerably before the big man lowered it again. "You know much about this here Brazos Devil, Custis?" he asked.

The grin disappeared from Longarm's face as he said, "Enough to be a mite worried about being out here after dark."

Catamount Jack gave a braying bark of laughter. "A big

fella like you, a lawman and all, and you're scared of some critter skulkin' around in the dark?''

"According to what I've been told, the Brazos Devil is suspected of killing four men. Ripping them apart with its bare hands or paws or whatever, in fact. But the real reason Thorp offered that bounty is because he thinks the thing might have carried off his wife.''

"Why in the world would a critter do that?'' Lucy asked. "You figure the Brazos Devil wanted to lay with the woman?''

Longarm wasn't surprised by the blunt nature of Lucy's question. He was convinced she was probably pretty well versed in the ways of the world. Likely she hadn't been shielded from much while she was growing up. Nobody would ever mistake Lucy Vermilion for a hothouse flower.

"I don't know if the Brazos Devil had anything to do with Mrs. Thorp's disappearance or not,'' he replied honestly. "There's a chance that an outlaw I brought in and one I had to kill a couple of days ago might be to blame for it. But somebody killed at least three men in a mighty bloody fashion quite a while before Mrs. Thorp ever vanished. Somebody—or some*thing*.''

"Saw me a critter like that once,'' said Catamount Jack, his voice more slurred now by the rye. Longarm hadn't drunk much from the bottle, and Lucy hadn't touched it at all, he realized now. Catamount Jack went on. "Sasquatch, some o' the tribes call it up yonder in the Northwest. *Ugly* critter. Never heard tell of 'em hurtin' nobody, though. Injuns say the critters are more scared o' people than people are o' them.'' He lifted the bottle for another drink, swaying a little as he did so. He was sitting cross-legged, so that kept him from toppling over, but Longarm could tell he was getting quite drunk.

"This fella Thorp,'' Lucy said, "what's he done about findin' the Brazos Devil 'sides postin' a bounty?''

"He and his ranch hands have searched all over his spread and on the other side of the river,'' Longarm said. "The marshal deputized some men and led a posse out too. They never found hide nor hair of the varmint.'' Longarm hesitated, then went on. ''Thorp's brought in some fancy Englishman, a big-game hunter. They're going out after the Devil tomorrow. I'm supposed to go with them.''

The last of the rye gurgled out of the bottle and down Catamount Jack's throat. ''Ahhhh!'' he said as he lowered the empty bottle. ''Well, we sure don't want no damned Englisher gettin' to the critter 'fore we do. We'll just have to beat 'em to the punch. We'll ride west an hour before sunup, daughter.''

''All right, Pa,'' Lucy said.

As drunk as Catamount Jack was, Longarm doubted if the man would even be capable of consciousness an hour before dawn, let alone going in search of the Brazos Devil.

In fact, Catamount Jack was swaying back and forth even more now, and he suddenly slumped over on his side. Almost instantly, loud snores began to issue from his mouth.

At the same time, Longarm thought he heard some shouting coming from the town, which was about five hundred yards distant. He wasn't sure about that, however, and besides, Mal Burley was in town. If there was trouble, it was the business of the local law to handle it. Longarm felt that he'd done his share for the night.

He inclined his head toward the slumbering Catamount Jack and asked, ''Does he do this very often?''

''Now and again,'' admitted Lucy. ''But don't you worry, Custis, he'll be sharp as a tack come morning. Nobody bounces back from a drunk as fast as my pa.''

''You sound like you're a little proud of him too.''

''Well, why shouldn't I be?'' she asked sharply. ''He's taken mighty good care of me. Maybe he never raised me the way most folks think a gal ought to be raised, but I always done just fine. And we've been happy. Ain't that worth somethin'?''

Longarm nodded solemnly and said, ''Yes, ma'am, Miss Vermilion, it is. It surely is.''

''You can call me Lucy.'' She stood up and went to one of

the packs they had unloaded from the mules. As she bent over it, Longarm couldn't help but notice the way the tight buckskin pants hugged her hips and thighs. She took a buffalo robe from the pack and came back to the fire. "Pull his feet around so they're not so close to the flames," she told Longarm.

He did as she requested, and she spread the robe over the sleeping form of her father. As she straightened and put her hands on her hips, she smiled down fondly at him. "He'll be all right just like that." Then she looked at Longarm and said, "You about ready to give me some lovin', Custis?"

He blinked in surprise, but managed to recover before he begged her pardon and asked her to repeat the question. Nodding toward Catamount Jack, he said, "In case you ain't noticed, Lucy, your daddy's sleeping right there."

"Hell, I know that. We'll go off in the trees a ways so we won't bother him. Anyway, Pa wouldn't care. I can tell he likes you, and he's a mighty good judge of what a fella's really like. Pa knows too that sometimes a body's just got to have some lovin'." She smiled down at Longarm and held out her hand toward him. "Come on, Custis. Don't make me hogtie you. 'Less, o' course, that's the sort o' thing you like."

Longarm growled, shook his head, and reached up to take her hand. He came to his feet in one lithe movement and pulled her into his arms. The evening had been much more eventful than he had thought it would be, and obviously it wasn't over yet.

"Reckon I'd better just show you what I like," he said.

They found an even smaller glade about seventy-five yards from the clearing where Catamount Jack slumbered peacefully. Longarm was a mite doubtful about leaving the older man there alone when a monster was supposed to be prowling the countryside, but Lucy assured him her father would wake up if the mules began raising a ruckus. And knowing mules the way he did, Longarm was sure no wild beast, not even one that was half-man, could come anywhere around without the mules pitching a fit.

There was only a tiny patch of moonlight in the glade, but it was enough for Longarm to watch appreciatively as Lucy pulled the buckskin shirt over her head and dropped it on the ground. Her breasts were gentle mounds crowned with dark, surprisingly large nipples. She took off her boots and slipped her buckskin trousers down around her hips, leaving herself naked. "The night air's cold," she said softly. "You'll have to keep me warm, Custis."

Longarm had brought along two more buffalo robes that Lucy had taken from the packs. He spread one of them on the ground. The other one they could pull over them. He had to shed his clothes first, though, so he hung his hat on a nearby bush and took off his coat.

"Let me," Lucy said, stepping closer to him. She reached out for the buttons of his vest and shirt.

Just looking at her while she was dressed, a fella might have thought it had been a while since she had gotten seriously acquainted with some soap and water. Now, though, divested of the smelly buckskins, she smelled clean and sweet, and Longarm wanted to plunge his face into her blond hair and breathe deeply of its fragrance.

He settled for standing there and looking at her as she commenced to undress him. She quickly removed his vest and shirt. Then her fingers moved to the buttons of his trousers. He was already hard and ready, and she made a little noise in her throat as she ran her palm over his groin, feeling the length and heft of him.

"My, oh, my, Custis," she said in a half-whisper. "I was right about you. I figured you for a big man."

"Was it my ears or my feet that gave it away?" he asked.

Lucy laughed. "Shoot, I don't put any stock in those old stories. I look in a man's eyes. I liked what I saw in yours, Custis, and I'm not just talking about this." She gave him another quick squeeze as she finished unbuttoning his pants.

Longarm gave her a hand, and it didn't take them long to get his trousers and boots off him. That left him in his summerweight long underwear; autumn wasn't far enough advanced to switch to the heavier undergarments yet. Lucy peeled them off him, letting his erect shaft spring free. She reached for it with both hands this time, trapping it in her soft, warm grip.

Longarm's hips instinctively flexed forward as Lucy wrapped her fingers around him. She sank down to the buffalo robe, still holding on to him. Longarm had no choice but to go with her.

As if he would have rather been anywhere else at this moment!

The night air *was* chilly, as she had said, but Longarm didn't really notice it. The heat from Lucy was more than enough to warm him. She drew him down on the robe beside her, then released him to reach for the other robe. As she spread it over them, she twisted around so that her face was pressed against his belly. Her tongue licked out into the mat of hair that covered most of the front of his torso, tracing a wet, white-hot trail across his stomach and abdomen to his groin. The top of her blond head bumped teasingly against his erection.

It was damned dark underneath that buffalo robe, but Longarm could smell the musk of her core as it moistened in anticipation. He reached out, touched the smooth flesh of her thighs. They parted, allowing him to run his fingertips over the even softer inner surfaces, moving closer and closer to the center of her. He felt her breath against his shaft, and her lips closed over the tip of the iron-hard rod at the same time as his fingers found the wet, fiery velvet of her slit. He slid two fingers into her, her muscles gripping them and pulling them deeper.

What she was doing to him with her lips and tongue was more than a solo on the French horn; it was a whole damned symphony. Longarm groaned as she opened her mouth even wider and took in more of him. She cupped his sac with one hand and rolled the tender little orbs back and forth, then used a fingertip to trace the little ridge of flesh beyond it. Longarm wanted to repay the oral favor she was bestowing on him. He leaned closer to her, parted her lower lips with his fingers, and began kissing and licking her, throwing in an occasional thrust into her with his tongue that rapidly became maddening to her. Lucy's hips pumped back and forth, and he could feel her hot breath coming more quickly on his shaft as she laved it with her tongue.

He wasn't sure how long the two of them drove each other crazy that way, but a fella couldn't go on like that all night. Finally, when he knew he couldn't stand much more, he reached for her shoulders and pulled her around so that they were facing each other again, even though they couldn't see each other in the dark. Longarm felt a sharp sensation of loss when she took her mouth away from his groin, but it was worth it when she began kissing him. Her legs straddled him, and neither one of them had to reach around and tuck him into her. It went in as natural as you please, as if it was meant to be there. Lucy settled back, filling herself with him, and she gasped against his mouth as the tip of his shaft butted against the very end of her passage. He was as deep in her as anyone could possibly go.

Her hips began to pump again. His organ slid in and out of her, and though she had been wet to start with, in a few moments she was well and truly drenched. She was breathing rapidly, and Longarm's pulse was pounding a mile a minute too. He lifted his head and found one of her nipples with his mouth. The nub of flesh was extremely erect. Longarm sucked it between his lips and ran his tongue along the corona of pebbled flesh surrounding it. Lucy gave a soft little cry.

She grabbed his shoulders as if she was holding on for dear life when her climax gripped her a moment later. Maybe she was afraid that otherwise the power of it would wash her away. Her spasming set Longarm off, and he lifted his hips from the buffalo robe to drive himself all the way into her again. Shudder after shudder shook him as he emptied himself into her in scalding bursts. Seconds drew out into minutes, minutes into hours, hours into days.

"The little death," Longarm had heard it called. It would

sure as hell do until the real thing came along.

He slumped back after his final convulsion had seized him. Every muscle in his body—well, nearly every muscle—was limp. Lucy seemed to be pretty much the same way. She had collapsed on his chest, and he could feel her heart thudding against him. She took in great breaths of air. Longarm knew how she felt. It seemed like a month since he'd had any air in his lungs.

After a few minutes, Longarm was able to speak again. "Reckon we're gonna live?" he asked.

"I . . . I don't know. I reckon I could . . . die happy . . . right about now . . .'cept for one thing."

"What's that?"

"We wouldn't be able to . . . do it again."

Longarm laughed. He stroked his hand down the smooth line of her back to the swell of her hips, then caressed her bottom, kneading the firm globes. She snuggled against him.

"I'm sure glad I met you, Custis Long."

"So'm I."

"You're better'n any ol' Brazos Devil."

That comment brought Longarm back at least part of the way to reality. And as it did, something bothered him, some nagging little annoyance that he couldn't quite grasp.

Before he could think about it anymore, Lucy bent her head and started tonguing his nipples, which was more than a little distracting. Longarm couldn't bring himself to ask her to stop just so he could think about things for a while, so he told himself to worry about it later. For the time being, he was content to enjoy what she was doing to him. He reveled in the languorous contentment that washed over him.

Then it all went away when he realized what he had heard earlier. He had little or no conscious memory of it now, but while they had been making love, a part of his brain that stayed alert had taken note of a particular noise in the night. Obviously, the sound hadn't represented an immediate danger; otherwise that facility of his—a sixth sense, he supposed you could call it for lack of a better term—would have warned him, no matter what he was doing. But still, it had been filed away in his brain, and now he recalled it.

The rapid hoofbeats of a galloping horse, heading west out of Cottonwood Springs.

Who would ride out of the settlement in the middle of the night, especially going hell-for-leather like that, with practically the entire countryside afraid of the Brazos Devil? Longarm knew he wasn't going to be satisfied until he found out the answer to that question.

"It ain't like I want to do this," he said to Lucy as he took hold of her head and tilted it up toward him, "but I got to get back to town."

"But Custis—" she began.

He kissed her, finding her lips with his in the dark. "Like it or not, we both have other reasons for being in this part of the country, Lucy, so we'd best get on about them. Maybe I'll see you tomorrow, since we'll all be scouting around in the same area looking for that critter."

"All right," Lucy said grudgingly. "But this better not be the only time you and me get to have some fun on a buffalo robe."

"I think I can promise," said Longarm, "that it sure won't be."

Chapter 10

Catamount Jack was still sleeping undisturbed; Longarm could tell that by the loud snores issuing from the old mountain man's mouth. He left Lucy at the campsite with a warning not to let the fire burn down too far during the night, then walked briskly back toward Cottonwood Springs.

He wished he had brought one of the horses out here. He could have covered the distance to town much more quickly if he had. As it was, it took him several minutes to reach the town, and the time seemed longer than it really was. Longarm had never thought of himself as the nervous type, but tonight he kept hearing noises that made him look over his shoulder. He had never known himself to be so spooked, especially not by the notion of a critter that might not even exist.

He found the town in an uproar. Groups of men stood around in front of the buildings, talking loudly. Longarm heard the words "prisoner" and "jail" as he walked past some of the men, and he stopped to grasp the arm of one of the townies.

"What's going on?" he demanded. "What's got everybody in such a state?"

The man pulled loose from Longarm's grip, then looked

more closely at him in the light that spilled through the windows of a nearby building. "You're that federal marshal, aren't you?" he asked.

"That's right," Longarm said.

"And you haven't heard about what happened?"

Longarm reined in his impatience. "If I'd heard, I wouldn't be asking," he said reasonably.

"I guess not." The man paused, obviously enjoying the dramatics of the moment, then said, "Your prisoner broke out of jail tonight."

Instantly, Longarm remembered the distant shouting he had heard while he was at the campsite outside of town. He recalled as well the hoofbeats of a galloping horse that had sounded a little later. That could have been Mitch Rainey fleeing Cottonwood Springs on a stolen horse, he thought.

"Where's Marshal Burley?" he asked tautly.

"Still down at the jail," the citizen replied with a nod of his head in that direction. "I hear tell Doc Carson's down there with him. The marshal got hurt somehow."

Longarm hoped the injury wasn't serious. He wasn't overly fond of Mal Burley, but he would never wish ill to a fellow lawman, as long as the star-packer was of the honest persuasion. Longarm thanked the townie for the information, then turned and headed for the jail as fast as his long-legged stride would take him.

Burley was seated behind the desk when Longarm walked into the office. Doc Carson stood beside the local lawman, probing with those delicate fingers at the back of Burley's head. Burley winced and said, "Hell, Doc, watch what you're doing. It feels like Rainey just about caved in my skull back there."

"I think you'll be fine, Mal," Carson said. "You've got a knot on your head the size of a goose egg, but other than that you seem to be all right. There's no sign of any brain fever."

Burley looked up and saw Longarm. A guilty scowl creased his face. "Hello, Long," he said. "I guess you've heard about what happened."

"Not enough," snapped Longarm. "How'd Rainey manage to get out of here?" Now that he knew Burley wasn't badly injured, Longarm wasn't in much of a mood to be sympathetic.

Burley grimaced again and said bluntly, "He played me for a fool. He started screaming and carrying on about how the Brazos Devil was right outside his window and was trying to get him. I unlocked the door and ran into the cell, thinking I might get a shot at the varmint, and then Rainey jumped me."

Longarm's features hardened, and trenches appeared in his cheeks. "You feel for that?"

"I said he played me for a fool, all right?" Burley stood up and came around the desk. He continued angrily, "Rainey put on a good act. He seemed just as crazy scared as you said he was out there by the river."

Longarm sighed heavily. It looked like he was going to have to give Burley the benefit of the doubt. "Maybe I would have done the same thing you did," he said—although he knew damned good and well that he probably wouldn't have. "What happened after Rainey jumped you?"

"He banged my head against the wall and gave me this," Burley said as he reached up to gingerly touch the lump on the back of his head. "I was knocked out for a minute or two. Not long, but long enough for Rainey to get my gun and lock me in the cell. I started yelling, but it was several more minutes before anybody came along to see what was wrong."

"And in the meantime, Rainey had stolen a horse and lit a shuck out of town," Longarm guessed.

Burley nodded. "That's what happened, all right. He grabbed one of the horses that was tied up in front of the saloon and headed out along the Fort Griffin road."

So more than likely that *had* been Rainey he had heard making his getaway, Longarm thought bitterly. If he had just been more alert . . .

No, under the circumstances, he had done pretty good just to hear the hoofbeats, he told himself more reasonably. The whole blasted world could come to an end and most men wouldn't notice at all if they were buried up to the roots in

Lucy Vermilion's sweet snatch, the way he had been.

"Moon'll be down in a little while," Longarm said, musing half to himself. "Wouldn't be able to do much tracking tonight . . ."

"It'd be best to wait until morning," Burley said. "I don't think you'd be able to find any trace of him in the dark. You'd just be wasting your time."

Longarm had to agree with him. It was frustrating, but the smart thing to do was to wait for daylight. "I was supposed to ride tomorrow with Thorp and that Englishman. Reckon you could go out there in the morning and tell 'em I'm busy with my own work, Marshal?"

Burley nodded. "I can do that. But you're liable to meet up with them yourself. Rainey'll probably hide out somewhere along the Brazos, since he knows that part of the country so well. Mr. Thorp and Lord Beechmuir might flush him out before they do the monster."

That was something to consider, Longarm thought. But in the morning, he would start by trying to track Rainey along the Fort Griffin road. There wasn't much traffic on that trail these days, and as long as there was no strong wind or rain, he thought he might be able to find the tracks left by Rainey when he fled Cottonwood Springs. It was worth a try, anyway.

"Maybe I'll run into them," he said noncommittally, but that was as far as he went.

"Rainey's a fool," Burley said. "I'd have taken my chances in jail, rather than going back out there."

"What do you mean?"

"The only weapon he has is my Colt, with five bullets in the cylinder." Burley shook his head. "If Rainey meets up with the Brazos Devil, that's not going to be nearly enough."

Longarm finally got to sleep that night, much later than he had originally intended, and despite his weariness he was awake and dressed an hour before sunup the next morning. Instead of his tweed suit, today he wore jeans and a denim jacket over a plain butternut work shirt, so that he looked more

95

like a cowboy. His boots, Stetson, and the cross-draw rig that carried his Colt were the same as always. He tucked a handful of cheroots into the pocket of his shirt before he went downstairs for a quick breakfast in the hotel dining room. He was one of the first customers in the place, since most of the hotel's guests weren't such early risers.

Longarm wouldn't have been either if he didn't have work to do. He washed down a plate of flapjacks, eggs, and steak with several cups of strong black coffee, and he felt alert and fairly human when he went down to the livery stable to saddle up the Appaloosa. The red glow in the eastern sky was growing as dawn approached.

He wondered if Catamount Jack and Lucy were still camped outside of town, but when he rode by the clearing just as the sun was peeking up over the horizon, he saw that the place was empty. Dismounting and bending down to check the ashes of the fire, he found them barely warm. Catamount Jack had said the night before that he wanted to ride out before sunup, and despite the monumental drunk on which the old man had embarked, it appeared he had met his goal this morning. Longarm returned to the road and scanned it for hoofprints in the growing light.

Only one set of tracks looked fresh enough to have been made the night before. The scare that the Brazos Devil had thrown into the countryside was going to come in handy now. If the Fort Griffin road had been carrying its normal amount of horse and wagon traffic, Longarm wouldn't have been able to track Rainey at all. This way, at least he had a chance.

He rode west as the sun climbed higher in the sky behind him. The morning was cool, and heavy dew sparkled on the grass alongside the road. Longarm heard a few birds, but other than that, the only sound was the clopping of the Appaloosa's hooves on the wide trail. Longarm's eyes were constantly moving, scanning the terrain around him.

For half an hour, he followed the tracks he believed had been left by the fugitive outlaw. Then, the thing that Longarm had worried about happened. The trail swung to the north, leaving the road. Longarm reined in and studied the tracks. It appeared that Rainey was angling toward the river. He probably meant to cross the Brazos and hole up in the even more rugged country on the far side. Longarm sighed. He was a decent tracker, but he knew Rainey's trail would not be easy to follow.

"Well, sitting here won't get us any closer to the fella who used to ride you, old son," Longarm said aloud to the Appaloosa. He heeled the spotted horse into a walk and left the road, heading north himself.

He was able to follow Rainey's trail for a couple of miles, but then the tracks led over a long, rocky ridge, disappearing on the hard surface. Nor did they reappear on the far side of the ridge. Rainey had used this natural feature to his advantage, and Longarm knew the only way to pick up the trail would be to ride back and forth along both sides of the ridge and hope he could spot fresh tracks. That would be a time-consuming task, and Rainey already had a big lead on him.

The other way he could proceed, crossing the ridge and continuing toward the river in hopes of picking up the trail farther on, was a big gamble, Longarm knew. But it might be his only chance of actually catching up to Rainey.

He urged the Appaloosa into a trot that carried it up and over the ridge.

Less than an hour later, he came within sight of the Brazos, catching a glimpse of it through the fold between two hills. So far he hadn't seen hide nor hair of Mitch Rainey, and Longarm's disgust was growing. It looked like he was in for another long, frustrating search, like the first one that had culminated in his near-fatal encounter with Rainey and the late Jimmy Lloyd. Not to mention that he still had the Brazos Devil and the disappearance of Emmaline Thorp to occupy his mind. He hadn't seen Rainey, but he sure hadn't seen any sort of monster either.

Longarm rode toward the river, maintaining his sharp-eyed alertness. Still, he had no warning when what sounded like an angry bee suddenly buzzed past his ear.

Instinct took over and sent him diving out of the saddle. He had heard way too many bullets coming close to his head over the years not to recognize the sound now. Since he hadn't gone out to the Rocking T to ride with Thorp and Lord Beechmuir as planned, he still didn't have a long gun, but the Colt was already in his hand when he hit the ground, for all the good it would do him. He rolled over a couple of times and powered into another dive that took him into a thick stand of trees. The Appaloosa scampered off several yards, evidently untouched by the shot but startled by his rider's abrupt reaction to it.

Longarm crouched behind the too-narrow trunk of a live oak and gritted his teeth against the curses that welled up his throat. That shot had come from a long way off, he knew, because he was vaguely aware that he had heard the sound of the rifle while he was already throwing himself out of the saddle. For a long-distance shot, it had come damned close to hitting him. Of course, it was possible it had been an accident, that whoever had fired the high-powered weapon hadn't been aiming at him at all. As far as he knew, Mitch Rainey didn't even have a rifle.

Of course, Rainey could have stolen one from a farm or ranch, Longarm thought. But it was more likely that someone else he knew to be in this part of the country had pulled the trigger. John Booth, Lord Beechmuir, had been bragging just the night before about how powerful his Markham & Halliday elephant gun was, and Longarm knew too that Catamount Jack packed a Sharps, which was fully capable of throwing a slug that far.

But why would either of those men, experienced hunters that they were, shoot at him? Longarm couldn't answer that question.

There had only been the one shot, and then silence had descended over the countryside again. Longarm wondered if it was safe to venture out. One thing was certain—he couldn't squat here in these trees all day.

He stood up and moved out of the thicket, calling softly to the Appaloosa as he did so. The horse had started cropping contentedly at the grass, and Longarm was able to catch him without any trouble. Longarm holstered his gun and swung up into the saddle. He twisted his head around, trying to figure out where the shot had come from. There was a wooded hill about six hundred yards away that would have made a good vantage point for the rifleman. Longarm squinted at it and wished he had the pair of field glasses he always carried in his saddlebags. Like all the rest of his gear, they had vanished with the gray gelding.

He thought he saw movement on the hill, but it was too far away to be sure of what he was seeing . . . or even if he was just imagining it. Still, Longarm pointed the Appaloosa in that direction and heeled it into a trot.

He covered the distance quickly, but by the time he reached the hillside, there was no longer anyone there. However, he found the prints of several horses—six or seven of them, in fact. That had to be Thorp's party, Longarm decided, although it was slightly larger than he had expected it to be. He followed the tracks around the shoulder of the hill.

Within fifteen minutes, he came within sight of them. There were seven people in the group riding across a meadow in front of him: Benjamin Thorp and two of his ranch hands, Lord Beechmuir, the two servants—and Lady Beechmuir. Longarm hadn't expected to see Helene Booth out here, but there was no mistaking the bright red hair underneath a yellow hat with a tall feather on it. The dress Helene wore was the same shade of yellow. Nobody was going to mistake her for a monster, Longarm thought—and that was a good thing under the circumstances.

He hailed them, and they came to a halt in the middle of the pasture. Longarm rode up to them and lifted a hand in greeting. "Howdy, folks," he said.

"Hello, Marshal," Thorp said. "I didn't think you were coming with us today. Mal Burley rode out to the ranch early this morning and told us about your prisoner escaping."

"Well, it looks like our paths crossed anyway, like I halfway expected they might. 'Pears that Rainey came in this direction when he lit out from the jail in Cottonwood Springs.''

Lord Beechmuir was wearing another one of those Wild West show costumes with a fringed and beaded jacket and tight leggings. His hat today was dark brown. He said to Longarm, ''We've seen no sign of your fugitive, Marshal.''

That was going to be Longarm's next question. Since Booth had already answered it, he asked another one. ''What about the Brazos Devil?''

Thorp sighed. ''No sign of him . . . or of my wife.''

''It's only been part of a day, old boy,'' Booth said. ''Don't give up hope.''

''Oh, I'm not,'' Thorp said with a shake of his head. ''I'll never give up hope.''

Longarm thought the declaration sounded a little hollow. Thorp was a man grasping at straws now, and they all knew it. Longarm said, ''I might as well ride along with you folks for a while, but there's one more thing I want to know first. Did any of you shoot at anything a little while ago?''

''I'm afraid that was me, Marshal Long,'' Helene said. ''I thought I saw the creature. The shot was a long one, but I took it anyway.''

Longarm looked directly at her and said, ''That was me you were shooting at, ma'am.''

Helene lifted a hand to her mouth and exclaimed, ''Oh, my God! Are you all right, Marshal?''

Lord Beechmuir asked anxiously, ''You weren't hit, were you?''

Longarm shook his head. ''No harm done,'' he assured them. ''But if you don't mind me saying so, your ladyship, that was a hell of a shot. You almost parted my hair for me at nearly six hundred yards.''

Helene's face was pale, washed out. She shook her head and said, ''I wouldn't . . . I never meant to . . .''

''It's all right, ma'am,'' Longarm said quickly. ''We all make mistakes.''

Booth looked at his wife but spoke to Longarm. ''I already made it quite plain to Lady Beechmuir that she should not

100

take any more shots without letting the rest of us know about it first. I promise you, Marshal, we were almost as startled as you."

"You don't have to be mean about it, John," Helene snapped. "I said I was sorry, and I'm sure Marshal Long knows that I meant no harm."

Lord Beechmuir said, "Well, I'm not sure why you decided to come along today anyway. I expected you to stay at Benjamin's ranch house."

"I've accompanied you on some of your other expeditions."

"Not when I was going after a creature like the Brazos Devil," Booth protested.

"Is that so?" Helene shot back at him. "I suppose it was safer when you were hunting that rogue elephant—"

"I said there was no harm done," Longarm cut in. "No point in fussing about it."

"Very well," Lord Beechmuir said stiffly. "Damn sportin' of you, Marshal. I might not be so forgivin' if it was me that my darlin' wife took a shot at."

Helene looked as if she wanted to say something else, but she fumed in silence. Longarm moved his horse alongside Thorp's, and the group started riding toward the Brazos again.

So it had been Lady Beechmuir who had fired that shot, Longarm reflected. Accidentally, of course.

But he remembered the way he had turned aside her advances the night before, and he recalled as well that old saying about the fury of a woman scorned.

Could be the Brazos Devil wasn't the only dangerous creature running around out here.

Chapter 11

They crossed the river a little before midday. Thorp led the way across the sandy streambed, warning the others to follow him closely so as to avoid the patches of quicksand. So far there had been no sign of the Brazos Devil, Emmaline Thorp, or Mitch Rainey. It was as if the rugged, wooded hills had swallowed up all three of them.

When the sun was directly overhead, Thorp called a halt. They were at the top of a grassy knoll with a good view of the countryside around them. As everyone dismounted, Randamar Ghote unwrapped a large bundle strapped onto his horse behind his saddle, revealing a wicker basket. Inside the basket were plates, glasses, a bottle of champagne, and several bowls of food. The silent Sikh, Absalom Singh, took a contraption from the pack on his horse that proved to be a folding table, and when it was set up, Singh brought out three folding stools as well. Longarm watched the servants setting up the meal with an amused look on his face.

"Not much like gnawing jerky and hardtack in the saddle, is it?" he asked Thorp.

The rancher shook his head. "Lord and Lady Beechmuir

are accustomed to a certain level of comfort, no matter where they are.''

Longarm could imagine the two servants carting around all this gear and setting it up in the middle of some African jungle. Booth and his wife seemed to take it all for granted. They sat down on the stools as Ghote spread the meal on the table, and Lord Beechmuir said, ''Please join us, Benjamin. My apologies, Marshal Long, but we only have one extra seat. You're certainly welcome to share in our repast, however.''

''Much obliged,'' Longarm said. He ambled over to the table and looked down at the food. It was simple fare— chicken, potatoes, corn on the cob, hunks of bread. But it was being served on fine china and washed down by champagne sipped from crystal glasses, here in the middle of nowhere. Longarm settled for a couple of drumsticks and a thick slice of bread. He sat down with his back against the trunk of a tree and stretched his legs out in front of him as he ate. He had brought supplies for his own lunch, but since Thorp's party seemed to have more than enough, he didn't mind joining them.

Lord and Lady Beechmuir chatted and laughed as if they were in some London drawing room while they ate. Thorp looked a little uncomfortable as he sat at the folding table with them. He might be a successful businessman now, but somewhere inside him was the frontiersman who had founded the Rocking T ranch before he ever became a banker, and had lived there in a rough stone house surrounded by cowboys. Longarm could tell that putting on all these airs bothered Thorp, but he was willing to tolerate almost anything if it might help his chances of finding his wife.

When the meal was over, Singh and Ghote cleaned up quickly and efficiently while Thorp and Lord Beechmuir smoked cigars. Longarm fired up one of his own cheroots and considered joining them, but he noticed Helene Booth slipping off into a growth of trees farther down the hill. She was just going to take care of some personal business, Longarm figured, but he still felt a twinge of worry. Privacy was all right, but with an escaped prisoner roaming these hills—to say nothing of a possible monster—Longarm decided somebody ought to at least stay within earshot of the lady. He strolled down the slope toward the oaks where she had disappeared.

Longarm hesitated when he entered the edge of the trees. He didn't want to embarrass Helene by stumbling onto something he shouldn't be seeing. He thought about making plenty of noise as he proceeded, scuffing his boots through the fallen leaves, maybe even whistling a few bars of that cavalry song about the big black charger. His lips were pursed to do just that when he suddenly heard low voices somewhere ahead of him in the trees.

A frown creased Longarm's forehead. One of the voices belonged to Helene; he was fairly sure of that. The other one he couldn't place. Low and silky, it belonged to a man. Longarm didn't recall seeing any of the other gents in the party following Helene into the trees. Maybe someone had come down here first to wait for her. No longer as worried about violating anyone's privacy, Longarm gave in to his curiosity and cat-footed forward.

He crouched behind a screen of brush as he spotted movement up ahead. Peering through the leafy undergrowth, he saw a flash of yellow and knew he was seeing Helene's gown. Longarm leaned forward and carefully moved aside a branch to give him a better view.

She stood there in a tiny clearing talking to Randamar Ghote. As Longarm watched, the little Indian servant reached inside his tunic and brought out a small bottle. "Your medicine, milady," he murmured as he handed the bottle to Helene.

She lifted it to her mouth and took a delicate sip, then shuddered and gave the bottle back to Ghote. "Thank you, Randamar," she said fervently. "I simply do not know what I would do without you to help me."

"It is my pleasure, milady," Ghote purred as he put away the bottle of medicine.

Longarm's frown deepened. He wasn't sure how Ghote had

104

managed to get down here in this grove of trees without being noticed, but he had already figured out how good Ghote was about sneaking around. The fella reminded Longarm of a Comanche during the time of the stalking moon: always around when you least expected him. This business about the medicine bothered Longarm too. What sort of illness ailed Lady Beechmuir? he wondered. She had certainly seemed healthy enough when she was trying to seduce him the night before.

He didn't have time to ponder the questions, because Helene and Ghote were leaving now, slipping out of the trees in somewhat different directions. Ghote would circle back to the camp around the hill, Longarm figured. That was probably how he had reached the trees in the first place. Longarm let them get a head start, then straightened to follow Lady Beechmuir.

He had only gone about a dozen feet when there was a faint rustling sound behind him. Before he could even start to turn around, an arm corded with muscle looped around his neck and clamped across his throat. He felt the pinprick of a knife's point underneath his jaw.

"Why do you spy on my mistress?" a deep voice asked.

Longarm stood still. He knew better than to commence thrashing around with a knife at his throat. The pressure on his neck eased enough for him to say, "Take it easy, old son. I'm not spying on anybody."

"Then what are you doing here?" the Sikh hissed in perfectly good English.

"What do you think I was doing?" Longarm didn't know how long Singh had been watching him, but he knew that if he hemmed and hawed the knife-wielding warrior sure wouldn't believe him. "I came down here in the trees to take a leak."

"To relieve yourself, you mean?"

"That's right. So I'll thank you to let me go and get that pigsticker away from my neck."

Longarm tried to sound suitably offended. Singh hesitated for a moment longer; then the pressure on Longarm's throat went away entirely, along with the knife. Singh stepped back and said, "When I saw you come into the trees, I thought you might intrude on her ladyship. My apologies, Marshal."

Longarm rubbed his throat briefly and nodded to the Sikh. "Didn't know you spoke our lingo so good. Hell, I wasn't even sure you could talk at all."

"I am a half-caste. My mother was British, and I was educated at the university known as Oxford. If I say little, it is because I have little to say."

"Most folks should be that smart," Longarm muttered. "Apology accepted, Singh. I don't reckon I can blame you for looking out for her ladyship. That's part of your job, after all."

Singh nodded curtly. "I will go back to the others."

"I'll be along directly," Longarm said. "Got to finish what I came down here for."

Singh nodded again and faded back into the trees, rapidly disappearing. He reminded Longarm once again of an Indian—the warpaint kind—just like his fellow servant Ghote. They were as lightfooted a pair as Longarm had ever run across, and he suspected that in a fight Singh would be more trouble than an armful of wildcats.

He just hoped he and the Sikh wouldn't wind up on opposite sides before this hunt was over.

Since he hadn't picked up Rainey's trail again, Longarm decided he might as well continue riding with Thorp's party. Once all the fancy trappings from lunch had been stowed away, they mounted up and rode northwest, generally following the course of the Brazos. The river was about a quarter of a mile to their right most of the time. Some of the landscape began to look familiar, and Longarm realized it wasn't far from here that he had finally met up with Rainey and Lloyd. The spot where Rainey had seen whatever spooked him so bad was also nearby. Longarm spoke up, saying as much to Thorp and Lord Beechmuir.

"Excellent!" Booth exclaimed. "I wanted to see that spot,

as you know, Marshal. The tracks you saw may still be there."

"They should be," Longarm said. "Hasn't been any rain since then."

They rode on, angling more toward the river now. They were making their way through one of the many stands of oak that covered the landscape when Singh suddenly spurred ahead of the others and held up a hand.

"Halt!" Lord Beechmuir said. "The Sikh has seen something."

So had Longarm. There was a dark shape on the ground about fifty yards ahead of them, on the edge of a small gully. At first Longarm wasn't sure what it was, but then he realized it was a body of some sort. Not human, though; it was too big for that.

"My God," Helene breathed. "What is it?"

"It's dead, whatever it is," snapped Thorp. "Come on."

Booth turned to his wife. "My dear, you stay here with Ghote and Benjamin's men. The Sikh will come with us."

Helene nodded, agreeing to stay back. Longarm and Thorp were already spurring forward. Booth and Singh rapidly caught up with them.

The ground around the body was darkly stained where blood had soaked into it. That was another way they knew the corpse didn't belong to a human being. No one had that much blood in his body. But a horse did, and as Longarm and the others drew closer to the grisly site, he could make out some dimly equine outlines. The horse had been ripped to pieces, though, so much so that it was barely recognizable.

"Good Lord!" Booth said as they reined in. A thick cloud of flies rose from the body of the horse and buzzed away angrily. "What could have done such a thing?"

"The Brazos Devil," Thorp said grimly. "This poor beast is ripped up just like the Lavery boys were. They didn't even look human anymore when the monster got through with them."

Longarm swung down from his saddle and knelt beside the gruesome remains. He touched the dark pool surrounding the horse. The blood that hadn't soaked into the ground had dried into a sticky, congealed mass. Longarm touched it with his fingertips and then rubbed them together, grimacing. "Probably happened yesterday," he said. "The horse wandered around for a day after he ran off the second time; then this happened to him."

"You recognize the animal?" asked Thorp.

Longarm nodded. "It's the gelding I was riding when I caught up to Rainey and Lloyd. There's not much hide left on the body, but what there is of it is gray. And that's my saddle." He sighed. The McClellan saddle had been ripped and torn and was soaked in blood. He wouldn't be using it again, nor anything in the saddlebags.

His Winchester wasn't in the saddle boot, though, and that was curious. He stood up and began walking in ever-widening circles around the horse, ignoring the curious stares of his companions. After a few minutes, he bent over and reached into a clump of brush. When he straightened, he was holding a rifle.

"Got some blood on the stock, but I can clean it off," he said. "The critter was curious enough to pull my rifle out of the boot, but when he realized it wasn't anything good to eat, he threw it away."

"He?" Thorp repeated.

Longarm shrugged. "Who knows? Those who have seen it say the thing's half-man, so I don't feel right calling him an it."

Thorp shook his head and said, "Anything that could do this to a horse . . . I'm not sure any part of it is human."

The man had a point, Longarm thought. He had seen horses pulled down by wolves and mountain lions that looked like this one, but he never would have dreamed that something which walked upright could do such damage with his—its—whatever—bare hands. Longarm felt a little shiver go through him.

While he searched for his rifle, he had also been looking for tracks. He resumed that search now, and several yards

108

away from the horse's body he found some. "Look here," he told the others. They joined him, and he pointed out the prints. The sharp claws on the gigantic feet had really gouged out the soft loam of the ground in places. Longarm said, "Those are the same sort of tracks I found the other day after Rainey started screaming."

All four of the men peered closely at the misshapen footprints. Singh muttered something that sounded like "Yeti."

"What's that?" Longarm asked.

"A legend in the part of the world Singh comes from," Lord Beechmuir explained. "High in the Himalayan Mountains, a creature supposedly exists that is part man and part monster, dwelling in the eternal snows of those slopes. I've often thought about going there and attempting to bag one of the beasts."

"Well, it doesn't snow very often in these parts, but I reckon the Brazos Devil could be a distant relation. What do you think, Singh?"

The expression on the Sikh's bearded face was fierce, but he shook his head. "It is not for me to say."

"Suit yourself." Longarm turned to Lord Beechmuir. "Think you can track the critter?"

"We shall certainly try. Are you going to continue to accompany us, Marshal?"

Longarm thought about it, then nodded. "Anytime anything's going on around here, the Brazos Devil seems to be somewhere close by. Maybe if we find him, we'll find Rainey too."

"And my wife," Thorp put in.

"Sure," said Longarm. "Mrs. Thorp too."

But in his heart, he no longer believed that. He had heard about what the Brazos Devil was suspected of doing to the Lavery boys and Matt Hardcastle, but hearing about those atrocities and actually seeing what had been done to this horse were two different things. He couldn't believe that any woman unlucky enough to fall into the hands of such a savage creature would still be alive weeks later.

109

And even if Emmaline Thorp was still drawing breath somewhere, it was unlikely that she was sane. Some female captives who had been carried off by the Comanches had lost their minds from the brutality with which the Indians had treated them. It had to be a lot worse being held prisoner by the Brazos Devil.

Longarm no longer doubted the existence of the creature. He had seen enough now to be convinced. Something was out here in these woods, something the likes of which folks had never run into before. Longarm had always been skeptical of such wild stories in the past, but now he believed.

And whether he wanted to admit it or not, he was a mite scared too. . . .

Chapter 12

Only a fool never experienced fear. Longarm had been scared plenty of times in his life, first as a farm boy in West-by-God Virginia, then as a soldier in the Late Unpleasantness. Once, when he was cowboying after the War, he had gotten caught in front of a stampede on a stormy night. He would never forget the rumble of hooves and the clashing of horns behind him, the noises blending with the roar of thunder and the crackle of lightning, as the crazed herd chased and closed in on him. If he hadn't had a good pony under him that night, he would have been mashed into the dirt of Indian Territory and left bloody and unrecognizable. As it was, he had been able to race out of the path of the stampede at the last minute, but the memory of that belly-churning, throat-clutching fear would always be with him, living a life of its own there in the back of his mind. Likewise, he had been in plenty of tough scrapes since he'd started riding for the Justice Department. There had been times when he fully expected to die and felt the fear any sane man would feel at that prospect.

But now the sensation crawling along his spine like a woolly-worm was different, and he sort of understood why some folks said the fear of the unknown was the greatest fear of all. Better the devil you know, the old saying said, rather than the one you don't.

Under the circumstances, it was mighty apt.

Longarm, Lord Beechmuir, and Singh followed the tracks of the creature while Thorp returned to the others to lead them in a circle around the horse's body. Booth did not want his wife to get too close to the slaughtered animal. Helene had already seen enough to upset her. They all rendezvoused on the far side of the gully and pushed on north.

A mile farther on, the trail turned back toward the river. The tracks led all the way to a section of bank that had collapsed so that it sloped gently down to the streambed. Longarm reined in and followed the prints with his eyes. They led across the sand to the channel of the Brazos, then disappeared.

"The beast must have gone there to drink after its meal," Booth said.

"But he didn't turn around and come back," grunted Thorp. "We'd be able to see the tracks." From his saddlebags he took a pair of field glasses like the ones Longarm had wished he'd had earlier. Thorp scanned the far side of the river for a few moments, then shook his head. "I don't see any tracks leaving the water on the other side. The thing must have waded upstream or downstream a ways before it came out."

"Reckon he was trying to throw off anybody following him?" Longarm asked.

"Is the creature that intelligent?" Lord Beechmuir put in.

Thorp shrugged. "Who knows how smart the bastard is? Maybe it just wandered off, or could be it's got enough animal cunning to be careful about leaving a trail. Maybe it's as smart as a man."

Longarm didn't think that was very likely, but regardless of the Brazos Devil's motivation, the trail was lost for the time being.

"We're going to have to split up," Longarm said. "That's the only way we can cover both directions of the river."

Thorp and Lord Beechmuir nodded, but Helene spoke up with an objection. "Is it safe for us to be separated like that

112

with such a creature on the loose?''

"Now you understand why I didn't want you to come," said Booth. "I didn't want to put you at risk. However, we have little choice in the matter. Benjamin, you and I will go downstream, and Marshal Long can go upstream. You'll come with me, of course, Helene.''

Helene's mouth tightened. "What if I don't want to?''

"See here!" Lord Beechmuir's eyes narrowed angrily. "I'll have no arguing. I want you to be safe, my dear, so naturally you'll accompany my party.''

With a determined shake of her head, Helene edged her horse closer to Longarm's. His mouth tightened as he saw what she was doing. She said, "I'll be perfectly safe with Marshal Long.''

"I'll not hear of it," Booth declared.

"Hold on," Longarm said. "There's no need to wrangle about this, your lordship. Lady Beechmuir ought to go with you and Mr. Thorp.'' He pointed with his thumb at Singh and Ghote. "I'll take these fellas. Mr. Thorp's riders can split up, one with each bunch.''

"No!" Helene objected. "Singh, you go with Lord Beechmuir and Mr. Thorp. Randamar can accompany Marshal Long and myself.''

Booth tugged on his Vandyke, evidently a habit he had when he was angry. "I don't like this. I don't like it a dashed bit.''

Thorp said, "While we're arguing, that monster's getting farther and farther away. We won't be apart for too long. Each group will ride along the river for two miles, then come back. If any of you spot the beast's tracks before then, fire two shots in the air, and the others will come to you. I'm sure Lady Beechmuir will be safe with Marshal Long, your lordship. One of your men and one of mine will be with them too.''

Booth took a deep breath and blew it out. "Very well. I agree that we're wasting time. Come along, Benjamin.'' He turned his horse and started back toward the south. Thorp, Singh, and one of Thorp's men fell in with him.

113

Helene gave Longarm a self-satisfied smile. "It appears that you and I are a team, Marshal. Shall we go?"

Longarm tried not to cuss under his breath. It was bad enough to be out here looking for an escaped prisoner and a varmint that could rip up a horse like that, but to be saddled with a proddy, horny Englishwoman under these circumstances was even worse. He was just glad that the separation would last only a little while; then Helene would be back with her husband and Lord Beechmuir could worry about her.

"All right," he said, not allowing his voice to reveal what he was feeling. "Let's go."

The channel of the river wandered back and forth across the wide streambed. Longarm sent Randamar Ghote and the Rocking T rider, whose name was Benson, across to the eastern side of the Brazos, while he and Helene Booth rode along the western edge of the stream. All four of them remained in the streambed itself, watching closely for tracks leaving the water.

As he rode, Longarm thought about a book he had once read by James Fenimore Cooper. Cooper's hero Natty Bumppo had been in a situation sort of like this, and he had solved the problem by diverting the stream so that he could see the tracks his quarry had left underneath the water—as if such tracks wouldn't have been washed away long before ol' Leatherstocking ever came along to look for them. It just went to show that people didn't always know what they were writing about, but Longarm supposed that was all right as long as they spun a good yarn.

"Do you think we'll find Mr. Thorp's poor wife still alive, Marshal?" Helene asked, breaking into Longarm's thoughts.

He shrugged his broad shoulders. "Hard to say, ma'am. I never ran up against anything like this before. After what I've heard about the things the Brazos Devil's done in the past . . . and after seeing what happened to that poor horse . . ." He left the sentence unfinished, letting Helene draw her own grim conclusions.

"Yes, it was dreadful, wasn't it? Still, I'm sure John will

114

be able to find the beast and kill it. Despite his other failings, he *is* quite a hunter." Helene paused, then went on. "I really am sorry about shooting at you earlier. I had no idea——"

"That's all right, your ladyship. No need to apologize again."

"Perhaps not, but I'm quite distraught about it. I wish there were some way in which I could . . . make it up to you, so to speak."

Longarm looked over at her, saw the lascivious glow in her eyes, and had no doubt what she was talking about. "You don't have to make anything up to me," he said gruffly.

"Oh, but I'd like to."

He recalled what she had said the night before about regarding him as a challenge, and he almost wished he had stood firm about her going with her husband when the group split up. He had no patience for senseless wrangling, though, and that was what the discussion was turning into. With a frown on his face, he turned his attention to the streambed and watched intently for any sign that the Brazos Devil might have left behind.

The river twisted and turned, and Longarm and his companions had just gone around a sharp bend when he spotted something up ahead. "Hold on a minute," he said to Helene. He motioned to Thorp's man, Benson. "You and Ghote stay here, Helene, whilst Benson and me take a look at this."

Benson's horse kicked up water as he splashed through the shallow river to join Longarm. They rode forward carefully, not wanting to spoil any of the footprints Longarm had seen. As they drew closer to the tracks, Longarm's pulse sped up. The prints were unmistakable. The Brazos Devil had left the water here and headed toward the western bank.

Longarm reined in with Benson beside him, then leaned over in the saddle to study the tracks more closely. As he did so, he heard those sounds again, the buzz of a giant bee and a sharp whip crack, much closer this time. They were followed closely by a thud and a grunt of pain. Longarm turned his head in time to see Benson tumbling from the saddle.

Longarm didn't waste any time. He wheeled the Appaloosa and yelled "Go!" at Helene and Ghote. "Get out of here!" He slapped the spurs to his mount, sending the animal leaping ahead.

Another bullet whipped past Longarm as he turned his head to check on Benson. The Rocking T puncher was lying face-down in the muddy water at the edge of the river. The first shot must have killed him instantly, Longarm thought.

Helene and the Hindu servant were looking at him with their mouths open in dumbstruck amazement. Longarm gestured frantically at them. "Ride, damn it, ride!" A third shot rang out, and to his left, the bullet struck the water with a splash.

The shots were coming from the trees along the western bank of the river. Longarm jerked out his Colt and twisted in the saddle to throw a couple of shots in that direction. He didn't expect to hit anything, but maybe he could distract the bushwhacker. The gunman was using a shorter-range repeater, probably a Winchester or an old Henry rifle, instead of a Sharps or a high-powered British elephant gun. Longarm thought again about Mitch Rainey.

Helene and Ghote had finally gotten it through their heads that they were in danger. Awkwardly, they pulled their horses around and started riding south. The soft, sandy bed of the stream didn't make for very good galloping, unfortunately. Longarm, who had the Appaloosa under better control, swept up beside them. "Head for the east bank!" he shouted at them, motioning with his free hand as he did so. The east bank of the river was more sparsely wooded than the west side, but there were enough trees there to give them some cover. Long-arm thought the ambusher would likely give up on the attack if they could get out of this streambed.

He triggered another shot toward the west bank, even though he knew he was far out of handgun range by now. Water splashed high around the hooves of the horses as Long-arm and his two companions veered toward the east bank. Once they left the Brazos, the bank on that side was consid-erably closer due to the twisting of the channel. Longarm started to think that they might make it.

That was when a giant fist slammed into the side of his head and sent him spinning out of the saddle into a pool deeper and blacker than any in the Brazos River.

Mitch Rainey let out a cackle of triumphant laughter when he saw Longarm fall. He worked the lever of the Winchester he had stolen from a farmhouse downriver that morning. The old man who had been breaking up a field to plant winter wheat had been friendly when Rainey first rode up, passing the time of day with the outlaw and even offering him a smoke. Rainey had accepted gratefully since he no longer had the makin's himself, and after a deep draw on the quirly, he had slipped Mal Burley's gun from behind his belt and shot the old fool in the head. He'd left the dead farmer facedown in the field and ransacked the nearby cabin, finding the Winchester, three silver dollars, and some food. Then he had struck out north along the river on the horse he had stolen in Cottonwood Springs.

Setting up the ambush had been dumb luck, but that kind was as good as any, Rainey thought. He had settled down for a short siesta, but voices from the river had awakened him. His heart had pounded in excitement when he peered through the brush along the riverbank and saw Longarm riding along beside the channel with some redheaded woman. A damned nice-looking woman too, Rainey had thought, even though the riders were too far away for him to make out many details. There were a couple of other men with them, a cowboy and a fella with a rag tied around his head. Rainey had never seen his like before, but he wasn't worried about that. What he wanted to do more than anything else was kill that son of a bitch Custis Long.

He would have gotten Long with the first shot, Rainey knew, if the lawman hadn't bent over to look at something in the streambed. The bullet had taken down the cowboy instead. That was all right; Rainey figured he'd have to kill all four of them before he was through. He shifted his aim as Longarm

117

and the others fled, feeling a fierce exultation when the marshal spun out of the saddle. Rainey couldn't tell how badly Long was hit, but he intended to put another bullet or two in the bastard just to make sure he was dead before picking off the lawman's slower-moving companions.

Rainey lined the sights of the Winchester on Longarm's still form and took a deep breath, ready to take up the slack on the rifle's trigger. Before he could do so, however, a deep boom sounded somewhere on the far shore and something slammed into the trunk of the tree Rainey was crouched beside. Splinters stung his face, and he fell to the side, as much from shock and surprise as from pain.

Blinking furiously, he looked up and saw the huge hole that had been gouged from the trunk of the oak. It looked almost like a cannonball had struck it. If the slug had been six inches to the right, his head would be blown to hell now and blood would be spurting from the stump of his neck. From the sound of the shot and the damage the bullet had done, he guessed the rifleman on the opposite bank was using a Sharps buffalo gun.

Scrambling back onto one knee, Rainey lifted the Winchester and searched for some sign of the man with the Sharps. He spotted a wisp of gray powder smoke drifting through the air above some brush. A glance at the riverbed told him that Longarm still hadn't moved. The woman and the other man were still heading toward the far shore, although the woman looked back anxiously over her shoulder at the fallen lawman. They could wait, Rainey decided. He still had twelve shots left in the Winchester. He would use them to pepper that clump of brush where the man with the Sharps was concealed. He was confident that the son of a bitch hadn't had time to reload.

Before Rainey could fire, another blast boomed from the eastern bank. Rainey was driven backward, and for one awful moment he was sure he had been hit. He was dead, a fist-sized hole punched through him by the monstrous slug, and his brain just didn't know it yet. He couldn't feel anything, especially in his hands and arms.

Then the pain started and he realized he was still alive after all. His arms cramped and spasmed and he gritted his teeth against the agony rippling through them. He looked around and saw the Winchester lying on the ground nearby, its barrel and breech ruined. The shot from the Sharps had struck the rifle, he realized, and once again it was pure dumb luck that the slug had been deflected enough to miss him. It could have just as easily ripped on through him.

A third shot crashed heavily through the air. Rainey *knew* that one had come too quickly. There had to be two enemies over there, each with a Sharps. Alternating shots as they were, they could throw almost as much lead as a lone gunman with a repeater. With the stolen Winchester now useless, Rainey didn't need anyone to tell him that the odds had shifted dramatically against him.

The pain in his arms, a result of the impact from the slug striking the weapon he had been holding, was beginning to ease a little. Rainey was able to put a hand down to balance himself as he scrambled to his feet. He turned tail and ran. Only a pure damned fool would go up against a pair of Sharps like that while armed only with a handgun.

More of the heavy slugs ripped through the trees around him as he fled, but none of them found him. His horse was about fifty yards back from the river. Rainey stumbled up to the animal, jerked loose the reins he had looped around a sapling, and vaulted into the saddle. He slammed his heels into the horse's flanks and gasped, "Let's get out of here!"

At least he had the satisfaction of knowing that Long was probably dead, he told himself. The federal marshal had certainly fallen like a dead man. Rainey's furiously thudding pulse settled down a little as he left the river behind. A Sharps rifle had a hell of a range, but those two on the other side of the Brazos would be shooting blind now. He was well out of sight.

He sent the horse up the slope of a small but fairly steep

hill. Just before it reached the crest, the horse suddenly shied to one side, then reared up on its hind legs and pawed the air with its front hooves as it whinnied shrilly in fright. Rainey grabbed for the saddlehorn to keep himself in the saddle, and hauled down on the reins with the other hand, sawing cruelly at the animal's mouth with the bit in an effort to bring it back under control. "Damn it!" he yelled. "Settle down, blast you—"

The horse leaped into the air, utterly terrified and desperate to get away. Rainey felt his grip slipping as his mount twisted frantically. He yelled another curse and kicked his feet free of the stirrups. If the horse bolted, he didn't want to be dragged behind it. The ground came up to meet him, slamming into his back and knocking the breath from his body.

Gasping for air, Rainey rolled over onto his stomach. He heaved several huge breaths into his lungs and tried to get his hands underneath him so he could push himself up onto his knees. He had to get after that crazy horse and catch it before it went too far.

The shadow that loomed over him made him freeze.

Rainey forgot about being out of breath. His body—and time itself—seemed to come to a grinding halt. All he was aware of was the massive shadow . . . and then the stench, worse than anything he had ever smelled before.

With near-infinite slowness, Mitch Rainey lifted his head so that he could peer up at the thing standing over him. Rainey's eyes seemed nearly as big around as saucers.

And then he began to cry. . . .

Chapter 13

Longarm woke to the crackling of flames and the smell of smoke and wondered if he was in hell. He took a deep breath, even though it pained him, trying to decide if the smoke smelled of brimstone. Nope, he decided, it wasn't likely he was in Hades. Not unless old Beelzebub was brewing up a pot of Arbuckle's.

He tried to lift his head, only to have the world start spinning backwards on him. A soft groan came from his mouth as he let his head ease back onto the softness underneath it.

"Better just take it easy, Marshal," a familiar voice said somewhere above him. "That was quite a knock on the head you took. Good thing your skull's so danged thick."

"So . . . so I've been . . . told," Longarm rasped. His throat was dry and painful, his voice hoarse.

He felt something at his mouth, opened his lips, and blessed coolness flowed down his throat. His first impulse was to gulp at the water, but whoever was holding the canteen took it away after much too short a moment to suit Longarm.

"Not too much," the woman said again. "You'll make yourself sick."

He had already figured out that his head was pillowed on a

female lap. He pried his eyes open, wincing against the garish light from the campfire, and looked up into the face of Lucy Vermilion. She smiled at him.

"The boy's awake, is he?" That booming question could have only come from Catamount Jack, Longarm knew. "So he ain't dead after all."

"Course not," snorted Lucy. "I told you he'd be all right, Pa. That bullet just grazed him."

Catamount Jack moved into view, peering down at Longarm with a curious look on his grizzled face. "How you feel, son?" asked the old mountain man.

"I've been better," Longarm replied, his voice clearer now but still a little weak.

"You'll be all right," Lucy told him. "I reckon you've got what they call an iron constitution."

Longarm's constitution felt more like tinfoil right about now. He managed to lift a hand and touched his head, or tried to anyway. All his fingertips found was a thick bandage wound around his skull. He figured he must look sort of like one of those servants.

That thought made him remember what had been happening when he was shot out of the saddle, and he said anxiously, "Lady Beechmuir . . . is she all right?"

"I'm fine, Marshal," said Helene Booth's voice in reply. Her pale face swam into Longarm's view as she looked down at him in concern. "The question is, how are you?"

Longarm noticed the glance that Lucy Vermilion sent up toward the Englishwoman. It was none too friendly, he judged, and he wondered if Helene had been trying to lord it over the younger woman. He suspected Helene would be biting off more trouble than she realized if she did that.

He answered her question by saying, "I'm all right, ma'am. Lucy, help me sit up."

"You ought to rest," Lucy said.

"Marshal Long made a reasonable request," Helene declared haughtily. "Please assist him." Her tone made it clear that she considered Lucy just as much a servant as either Ghote or Singh.

Lucy's mouth tightened, but she did as Lady Beechmuir asked. Another wave of dizziness washed over Longarm as Lucy helped him sit up. Nausea that was even worse than he had experienced after eating that bad steak gripped him for a moment. But it passed quickly, and with Lucy's strong arms supporting him, he was able to remain sitting up.

He could look around the camp then, and he wasn't surprised to see Benjamin Thorp, John Booth, and the two servants clustered by the fire. The Rocking T hand who had survived the afternoon, a fella called Randall, was nearby tending to the hobbled horses. Everyone else was looking at Longarm with expectant expressions on their faces, and he realized they were waiting for him to say something.

"Much obliged to all of you for helping me out," he managed with a nod. "I reckon I can guess what happened."

"Lucy an' me come along when some sidewinder was tryin' to bushwhack you," said Catamount Jack. "We threw some slugs 'cross the river and run him off."

"Had to be Rainey," Longarm said grimly.

"What about the Brazos Devil?" Thorp asked from the other side of the fire.

Gingerly, Longarm shook his head. The memory of everything that had happened over the past few days had flooded back into his mind by now, and his mental processes were fairly clear as he said, "I haven't heard any mention of the Brazos Devil ever using a Winchester, have you?"

Thorp inclined his head in acknowledgment of Longarm's point. He said, "You're probably right. But if Rainey ran into the Devil before and was so scared he nearly shit his pants—pardon me, ladies—why would he come back into this part of the country?"

"He knew I'd be on his trail," Longarm said, "and he knows this Brazos River country better than anywhere else. I reckon he figured he could hide out easier here and avoid running into that monster at the same time." Longarm pointed to the coffeepot sitting in the embers at the edge of the fire. "I could use a cup of that coffee."

Ghote poured it for him and brought it to him, bending gracefully to hand it to him. Longarm recalled the "medicine" he had seen the servant giving to Lady Beechmuir, and wondered what the stuff was. If it cured headaches, Longarm could use some right about now to go with the coffee. He wasn't going to ask about it, however, knowing from the way Helene had acted that she didn't want her husband to know about what she was taking. Could be too that it was laudanum, and Longarm didn't want any part of that. He would just put up with the pounding in his skull, he decided as he sipped the strong black brew.

Longarm shifted his gaze to Catamount Jack and Lucy. "Did either of you get a good look at the bushwhacker when you opened up on him?"

"Nope," Lucy replied. "Pa and me heard the shootin' and rode over to the river to see what was goin' on. We got there just in time to see you go tumblin' out of your saddle."

Catamount Jack took up the story. "Saw powder smoke comin' from the trees on the opposite bank, so we unlimbered our Sharpses and started throwin' lead. Don't know if we ever hit the sumbitch or not, but a couple of minutes later we heard hoofbeats 'cross the river. Reckon he lit a shuck out o' there once he saw what he was up against."

"It was Rainey," Longarm said with a nod. "Had to be. Nobody else had any reason to ambush us."

Thorp said, "Lord Beechmuir and I arrived a few minutes later. We had heard the shooting, of course, and we abandoned the search and came as soon as we could. When we got there, I thought you were dead, Long, just like poor Benson. There was blood all over your head." He pointed at Lucy with a thumb. "This young lady was determined to patch you up, though. She said she wasn't going to let you die."

Longarm looked at Lucy, who seemed a bit uncomfortable with that revelation. "I could tell you'd be all right," she said gruffly. "You ain't the first fella I ever saw who'd been creased by a bullet."

"Hell, the gal's doctored me back to health when I was a heap worse off," Catamount Jack said, pride in his voice. "Why, I remember one time up in Wyoming when I got to rasslin' with this ol' silvertip grizzly—"

"Nobody wants to hear about that, Pa," Lucy broke in. "What's important is that Marshal Long will be all right if he takes it easy for a few days."

Longarm wasn't sure he *had* a few days in which to rest. Not with Rainey still on the loose, Thorp's wife still missing, and a monster still roaming around the area. By morning, he would have to be able to ride again, concussed or not.

He looked at Thorp and asked, "Did you find those tracks in the riverbed?"

Thorp nodded, a look of excitement on his face. "We saw them, all right. Once we'd buried Benson and set up camp and Miss Vermilion was tending to you, Lord Beechmuir, Catamount Jack, and I went to take a better look."

Somehow, the idea of Catamount Jack and Lord Beechmuir hunting the creature side by side struck Longarm as a little funny, but once he thought about it, there were some similarities between the two men. Both of them were hunters, both devoted to stalking their quarry through just about any kind of wilderness.

"Unfortunately, we lost the trail on the other side of the river," Lord Beechmuir said. "Damn bad luck, if you ask me."

"The varmint went traipsin' over a big stretch o' limestone up on one of them cliffs overlookin' the river," said Catamount Jack. "Couldn't pick up his trail again. He's a slippery cuss, that'un."

Longarm heard the frustration in the mountain man's voice. He knew the feeling. To have had Mitch Rainey locked up in jail, only to lose him again . . . that was the kind of thing that would have had Longarm tearing his hair out by the roots had he been the type to give in to such emotional displays.

Thorp took a cigar from inside his coat, lit it with a flaming twig from the fire, and blew out a cloud of smoke. "We're going to join forces with Vermilion and his daughter," he said. "I brought along enough supplies to last for several days. I'm not going back until I find that beast and find out what happened to my wife. But I can send Randall back to town with you and Lady Beechmuir if you want, Long."

"Wait just a moment," Helene protested before Longarm could say anything. "I haven't asked to return to town, have I?"

Her husband snorted. "For God's sake, you were almost killed this afternoon, Helene! Not only do we have to contend with the monster, whatever it may be, but now there's that man Rainey to worry about. No, I insist you return to the town with Marshal Long."

"I haven't said *I* was going back," Longarm snapped.

"You're in no shape to go gallivanting around over the countryside," Lucy told him.

Longarm shook his head. "I'll be fine. I've got a stake in this hunt too."

"If we find Rainey, we'll bring him back to Cottonwood Springs," offered Thorp.

"I don't reckon my boss would be too understanding happen I should tell him I sat around town while a bunch of civilians tracked down an escaped prisoner for me," Longarm said dryly. "No offense, Mr. Thorp, but you don't know Chief Marshal Billy Vail the way I do."

Thorp shrugged. "I'm not going to argue with you. It's your head, Long."

"And I'm not going to argue either," Helene said. "I'm staying with the group, and that's final."

Booth seemed about to disagree some more with his wife; then an expression of resignation appeared on his distinguished features. "Very well," he said curtly. "I know that arguing with you, Helene, is much like arguing with the London fog. It does as it pleases, no matter how one rails against it."

126

Helene smiled smugly. "So very gracious of you, John."

At the moment, Longarm wasn't interested in the way they sniped at each other. The sickness in his belly had passed, and now he was conscious of how empty it was. "If there's any supper left, I could do with some," he said, and Randamar Ghote brought him a plate of bacon, biscuits, and beans. Simple fare, but Longarm had rarely tasted better. The fancy china, the folding table, and the champagne were nowhere in sight tonight. Obviously, the events of the afternoon had made everyone in the party realize that this was serious business, not some sort of lark. Longarm hoped that Lord and Lady Beechmuir, especially, would remember that.

While Longarm was finishing the food, Thorp said, "We'd better take turns standing guard tonight. I don't want that monster stumbling over our camp in the dark . . . although if he did, that'd save us the trouble of hunting him down."

"Capital idea, Benjamin," Lord Beechmuir agreed. "There are six men, not counting the marshal, who should be exempt due to his injury, of course. I suggest we form teams of two men each. Singh and I would be glad to take the first turn, then Ghote and your man Randall could have the second part of the night, leaving yourself and Mr. Vermilion to finish the task."

Thorp was nodding when Lucy said, "Wait just a darned minute. I can stand guard as well as any man."

"'Tain't necessary, daughter," Catamount Jack said. "What Lord Beechmuir says makes sense."

Longarm was feeling better now that he had eaten, so he spoke up. "I don't mind taking a turn. I had a nice long nap—even though it wasn't my idea."

"There's a big difference in sleepin' and bein' knocked unconscious," Lucy pointed out. "You ought to rest, Marshal."

Longarm set his empty plate aside and fished a cheroot out of his shirt pocket. This bunch couldn't do *anything* without talking it to death first, he realized. The whole lot of them should have run for Congress and gone to Washington. But he just said mildly, "If you're worried about me, Miss Vermilion, I reckon you and me could take the same turn. Then you could keep an eye on me."

"Well . . . it would only be for a couple of hours if there's four teams," Lucy said. "I reckon it'd be all right. We'll stand the first watch, though, so in case you get to feelin' poorly, we can wake up somebody else and let them take over."

"Fair enough," Longarm said with a nod, then looked around to see if everybody was in agreement.

No one objected, although Longarm thought he saw a definite look of disapproval in Helene Booth's eyes. He wasn't sure why she would care one way or the other, unless she still had her cap set for him and was jealous of the fact that Lucy would get to spend that much time with him. The way he felt, though, romance was sure as hell about the last thing on Longarm's mind, so Helene didn't have anything to worry about.

With the matter settled, everybody got ready to turn in except Longarm and Lucy. She poured another cup of coffee for him and one for herself, then sat down cross-legged beside him on the ground, her Sharps at her side.

Not surprisingly, Lord and Lady Beechmuir didn't just spread their bedrolls on the ground in plain sight of everybody else. The seemingly bottomless packs they had brought along yielded up a canvas tent, which Singh and Ghote set up with practiced efficiency. The tent wasn't large, but it was big enough for Booth and Helene. The two servants slept in the open, rolling up in blankets, as did Thorp and Randall. Catamount Jack, of course, was accustomed to having no roof except the stars, and within two minutes after he spread his buffalo robes and crawled into them, he was snoring loudly.

Longarm waited until it seemed that everybody was asleep, then stood up. Instantly, Lucy was on her feet beside him, worriedly putting a hand on his arm. "What are you doin', Marshal? If there's something you need, I'll be glad to fetch it."

"No offense, Miss Vermilion, but some things a fella's just got to do by himself," he said with a faint smile.

"Oh. Well, in that case . . ." She picked up his Winchester and handed it to him. "You'd better take this with you, and keep your eyes open."

"I generally do," Longarm assured her, not adding that when a man took a leak with his eyes closed, he sometimes wound up pissing down his boot.

He felt a little shakier than he let on, but he was able to circle the campfire and move off into the darkness beyond the ring of light. It took only a moment for him to realize that they were camped on a bluff overlooking the river. He could see a silver line of moonlight reflecting off the Brazos below. The night was full of sounds: the call of an owl, the rustle of small animals, the far-off howl of a coyote. The noise was a welcome reassurance to Longarm that nothing strange was prowling around at the moment. He would have worried more if the night had been quiet.

He tucked the rifle under his left arm, unbuttoned his trousers, and took care of the business that had brought him here, sending his stream arcing out over the edge of the bluff and letting it splash to earth some seventy or eighty feet below. When he was done he buttoned up again and started to turn around. He froze, then edged his hand toward the action of the Winchester when he saw a shadowy figure approaching him.

It took him only an instant, however, to realize that the person coming toward him was Lucy Vermilion. As she moved, she passed between him and the fire, some twenty yards away, and he saw her silhouette clearly against the flames. "What are you doing out here, Lucy?" he called softly. "I told you I'd be right back."

"I got to worryin' about you bein' so close to this bluff, Custis," she replied as she came up to him. "I was afraid if you got dizzy, you might topple right off of it."

"Well, I didn't," he told her as he took a step toward the fire. "We'd best get back to camp. We're supposed to be standing guard."

"In a minute," she said, moving so that she blocked his

129

path. She put a hand on his arm again and went on. "I've been thinkin' about you ever since last night, Custis. I know you ain't up to any slap-and-tickle tonight, but as soon as you're feelin' better . . . well, maybe I better just give you a sample of what you got to look forward to."

She came up on her toes and her mouth found his. Longarm's head still hurt and he experienced occasional spells of dizziness, but without hesitation, he put his free arm around her and pulled her tightly against him. Her lips opened and her tongue darted against his. He parted his lips to let her in. She probed wantonly in his mouth as her belly ground against his groin. Despite everything, he felt his staff hardening, and so did Lucy.

She took her mouth away and whispered, "I ain't a tease, Custis, I really ain't. But you ought to recuperate a mite before we really go at it again."

"You're right," Longarm agreed. "But we don't neither of us have to like it, do we?"

Lucy giggled, a somewhat surprising sound from such a self-reliant young woman. "We'd better get back to camp," she said. "I shouldn't be out here temptin' you. I just didn't want you to forget about what we had before . . . and what we'll have again."

"I'm not likely to forget," Longarm said fervently. "Not likely at all . . ."

Chapter 14

He had to be dreaming, Longarm thought as he woke later that night. He felt a hand at the buttons of his trousers, unfastening them. Soft, warm fingers stole inside the garment and caressed his organ through the long underwear for a moment, then unbuttoned the underwear as well so that his erect shaft could spring free of its confinement. Those fingers closed hotly around it.

Definitely not a dream, Longarm realized, but he was still half-asleep anyway, and the bullet crease on the head he had suffered was making it difficult for him to throw off the bonds of slumber. "Damn it, Lucy," he muttered under his breath. Obviously, she hadn't been able to wait after all. He hoped nobody else had noticed her slipping into the bedroll he had fashioned out of blankets borrowed from Thorp's supplies.

The fingers slid lightly up and down his stalk. Longarm let out a muffled groan of passion. His hips twitched involuntarily.

With the part of his brain that was functioning, he wondered what time it was. He and Lucy had stood guard over the camp until midnight, then woken up Lord Beechmuir and Singh and turned the duty over to them. Longarm forced his eyes open

131

and studied the stars he could see through the trees around the camp. From the look of those celestial timepieces, several hours had passed since he fell asleep. Randamar Ghote and the cowboy called Randall were probably standing guard now. Longarm sort of hoped so anyway. Despite Lucy's assurances otherwise the night before about how her father wouldn't care, Longarm didn't much cotton to the idea of Catamount Jack finding the two of them snuggled up together like this. It would be bad enough if they were discovered by one of the others.

Maybe he ought to just tell Lucy to go back to her own bedroll, he decided. He lifted his head, intending to whisper to her to do just that, when the warmth of her hand went away from his shaft and was replaced by an even greater heat.

Longarm's head flopped back and he groaned softly once again as lips closed sweetly around his shaft. He closed his eyes and gave himself over to the sensation. A wet, almost searingly hot tongue circled the head of the pole of quivering flesh. His hips thrust up again, driving more of his length into her mouth. She grabbed on with both hands and sucked harder. Longarm felt his climax building.

There was no turning back. The skillful ministrations of her lips and tongue brought him to the brink in no time. Her grip on him tightened as his seed boiled up and exploded out of him. She didn't pull her lips away, but instead swallowed greedily as he filled her mouth with the culmination of his passion. Spasms shook Longarm's entire body for a seemingly endless moment; then he slumped back, an irresistible lassitude sweeping over him. He was still weak from his injury, he knew, and Lucy had just about worn him out. He breathed deeply, trying to recover from the internal earthquake. His head didn't hurt at all, he realized, even though his pulse was pounding loudly inside his skull.

Suddenly, a disturbing thought occurred to him. He didn't *know* that was Lucy sharing his bedroll. Whoever had just given him that mighty nice French lesson had been little more than a mouth and a pair of hands. Soft hands, at that. Uncallused hands. The hands, say, of Lady Beechmuir or even that little Hindu, Ghote—

Longarm's eyes snapped wide open, and it was all he could do to keep from bolting upright with a shout. His pulse began to race even faster, but it wasn't from lust or excitement now. It was pure-dee fear that made him practically lunge toward the other person in the blankets with him.

Relief flooded through him as he touched long, silky hair. His fingers tangled in it, and he practically hauled its owner up closer to his head. With a chuckle, Helene Booth molded her naked body against him and said in a husky whisper, "Really, Custis, you don't have to be so rough. Unless, of course, that's the way you like it . . ."

"Lady Beechmuir!" Longarm grated. The tide of relief that had washed through him began to ebb, only to be replaced with anger. "What the hell are you doing here?"

The fire had burned down almost to ashes, but it still cast enough light for him to be able to see her face as she smiled and licked her lips. "I should think that would be obvious," she whispered. "Wouldn't you? And please, you simply must start calling me Helene. Especially now that we've—"

"Don't even say it!" Longarm hissed as he closed his eyes and grimaced.

"Why, Custis, you're acting like you didn't even know it was me who . . ." She stopped short, and her attractive features hardened in the dim light from the fire. "You *didn't* know it was me, did you?" she accused. "You thought I was that little whore Lucy!"

Her voice was getting louder with anger, and Longarm shushed her as quietly as he could. He lifted his head and looked around, not seeing Ghote or Randall anywhere nearby. He had spread his bedroll right on the edge of the circle of firelight, thank goodness, and that circle had shrunk even more in the time he had been asleep. Whoever was on guard duty needed to feed some more wood to the fire and build up the flames . . . but not until Longarm got Lady Beechmuir back into her tent!

133

"You'd better go on back where you belong," he told her quietly. "How'd you manage to sneak out of that tent without Lord Beechmuir knowing anyway?"

"Oh, John sleeps like a rock. Nothing ever disturbs him." Helene frowned. "And it's bloody well unfair for you to make me leave after what I did for you. The least you could do is return the favor." The frown turned into a lascivious smile. "I'll wager that mustache of yours tickles in the most delightful fashion."

"You'll never know," growled Longarm. "Now get on back where you're supposed to be, or I won't have any choice but to raise a ruckus."

"You wouldn't dare!" Helene gasped. "Why, you have more to lose by doing that than I do."

"I don't see how you figure that." Longarm didn't want this whispered conversation to continue, but short of physically booting her out of the bedroll, he didn't know what he could do other than try to talk some sense into her.

"Even if John knew about the two of us, he wouldn't do anything to me," she said, her voice utterly confident. "He can't afford to."

Longarm shook his head. "Don't reckon I follow you. Don't they have divorce courts in England?"

"Certainly they do, but John would never divorce me. You see, Custis . . ." She traced a fingertip through the thick hair at the opening of his shirt. "John may have the noble title, but *I* have the money in the family. If he were to divorce me, who do you think would pay for those hunting expeditions all over the globe?"

Longarm took a deep breath. He understood a lot more now. Booth had married Helene for her money, and she had married him for his title. A fair arrangement all the way around, especially for folks who didn't take their wedding vows any too seriously. But that didn't mean Lord Beechmuir would continue to overlook his wife's affairs if she started flaunting them in his face. Even if he couldn't do anything about Helene's wanton behavior, he might not look so kindly on her male

134

partners. He might even reach for that Markham & Halliday elephant gun.

Longarm didn't want any trouble like that, at least not until Mitch Rainey was either dead or behind bars again and the mystery of the Brazos Devil and Emmaline Thorp's disappearance had been solved.

"I'm not going to argue with you," he said sternly to Helene. "You go on back to your tent, and we won't say any more about this."

She stared at him in frustration and surprise. "You won't do anything for me?"

"Damn it, I can't! Or at least, I won't. I'm no saint, but I've always figured there's some things a fella just shouldn't do."

Helene glared at him. "You, sir, are a bounder!"

"Whatever you say, ma'am. Just get your noble little ass back where it belongs."

"Oh!"

He looked around worriedly, sure that somebody must have heard her angry exclamation, but nobody seemed to be stirring around the campfire. Catamount Jack's snores were as loud as ever, and the mound of buffalo robes near him that marked Lucy's bedroll was still and silent except for the regular rise and fall of her breathing. Thorp looked like he was asleep too, and there was still no sign of Randall or Ghote. Longarm was beginning to worry about that. He should have seen at least one of the guards by now.

Of course, the fact that they weren't around meant that Helene could get back in her tent unnoticed, if she ever left his bedroll. She was finally angry enough now to do that. She slipped out of the blankets and stood up, giving him a tantalizing glimpse of her nude body before she wrapped it in a blanket she must have brought with her. She glowered down at him for a second, then turned and stalked back toward the tent she was supposed to be sharing with her husband.

Longarm heaved a sigh of relief when she disappeared through the flap in the canvas. Maybe this little debacle wouldn't cause any more trouble than it already had.

Despite his weariness, he knew he wouldn't be able to go back to sleep until he figured out where Ghote and Randall were. Now that he didn't have to worry about Helene anymore, he realized that the whereabouts of the missing guards might be a much more important concern.

He tossed his blankets aside, climbed to his feet, and buttoned up his underwear and trousers. He picked up his Winchester and started circling the camp, moving as silently as an Indian and listening intently for any sound that might indicate trouble.

It wasn't a sound that made him freeze a few moments later, though, his hands tightening on the rifle. It was a smell.

The sharp, coppery smell of freshly spilled blood. A *lot* of blood.

For a long moment, Longarm listened even harder than he had before. As had been the case earlier in the night, the normal nocturnal sounds were all he heard. He took a deep breath. That was definitely blood he smelled, with an unpleasant tinge of human wastes mixed in with it. The scent of death, Longarm thought. He had smelled it too damned many times in the past.

Quietly, he moved deeper into the trees surrounding the camp, away from the direction of the river. That seemed to be the direction the smell was coming from.

The darkness was almost total, since very little of the light from the moon and stars penetrated the thick overhang of branches. Many of the trees were live oaks and still had their leaves, which blocked off that much more of the illumination. Longarm wished he could strike a match, but that would just make a target of him if anybody was waiting out there in the darkness.

Suddenly, his booted foot struck something soft. Longarm stopped in his tracks and grimaced. He knelt, holding the Winchester with his right hand gripping the stock and his index finger through the trigger guard. He reached out with his left hand and touched cloth. Moving his hand over the fabric, he found some buttons and decided it was a shirt. The man wearing it didn't move.

Then Longarm touched something wet and sticky and knew all too well what it was. His fingertips explored the stain, and his hand drew back involuntarily when he touched rapidly cooling flesh. He had felt the deep gash in the man's throat.

Somebody had carved this poor bastard a new smile.

Longarm figured he knew who the dead man was. From the style of the shirt, the dead man was dressed cowboy, and that meant he was Randall rather than Ghote. That explained where one of the missing guards was, but Longarm was still left with plenty of questions. Who had killed Randall, and why? Where was Ghote?

The murderer must have struck smoothly and quietly, Longarm thought, to have carried out his deadly mission without disturbing the night life around the camp. This killing, at least, couldn't be laid at the feet of the Brazos Devil.

Longarm straightened and backed away from the body. It was time to roust the others and try to find some answers.

He turned and started toward the dimly burning fire, but he had taken only a couple of steps when a soft voice said, "Marshal Long? What are you doing out here?"

Longarm stiffened and brought up the barrel of the Winchester. He eased off on the pressure just as he was about to pull the trigger of the rifle. "Damn it, Ghote!" he snapped. "That's a good way to get yourself killed!"

"What is wrong, Marshal?" asked the Hindu servant. Longarm could see the white turban wrapped around his head now. "I thought you were sleeping."

"I was," Longarm said. He didn't explain what had awakened him. "I woke up and saw you and Randall weren't anywhere around, so I got up to look for you. You shouldn't go off and leave the camp unguarded."

Ghote's voice was puzzled as he said, "But the one called Randall was here when I left."

"Where'd you go?"

"I thought I heard a noise, on the bluff over the river. I

went to look. Randall stayed behind to watch the camp. But when I returned after finding nothing, I saw that not only was Randall gone, but you were too.''

Longarm jerked a thumb over his shoulder. ''Randall's back there in the woods—with his throat cut. You wouldn't know anything about that, would you, Ghote?''

The little Hindu drew himself up stiffly. ''I have not neglected my duty, and I am not a killer.''

''We'll see about that,'' Longarm said, his voice cold and hard. ''Come on.''

Ghote didn't say anything else, but Longarm could almost feel the anger and dislike radiating from the man. He herded Ghote back to the fire and ordered, ''Throw some more wood on there. You shouldn't have let it burn down so low.''

Ghote complied while Longarm thought about what had happened. Everything could have occurred just as Ghote said. But the servant could be lying, might be trying to cover up his part in Randall's death by claiming that he had been investigating some mysterious noise.

Longarm knew from experience how quietly Ghote could move, and he had been instinctively suspicious of the man from the first.

Of course, Mitch Rainey was still out there somewhere too. Longarm wouldn't have put it past Rainey to lure the cowboy out of camp some way, then slit his throat. The fugitive outlaw could be trying to eliminate the party one by one.

About the only people Longarm could truly rule out as suspects in Randall's murder were himself and Lady Beechmuir, since they had been otherwise occupied when somebody was whittling on Randall's neck.

''Wake up, folks,'' Longarm said, raising his voice. Ghote had the fire burning brighter now, the flames leaping higher as the crackling noise from the burning branches also increased. ''Everybody wake up, we got trouble.''

Benjamin Thorp came floundering up out of his blankets with his six-gun in his hand. ''What the hell!'' he exclaimed. ''What's wrong, Long?''

Catamount Jack and Lucy Vermilion also emerged from their buffalo robes, snatching up their Sharps carbines as they did so. "Catch sight o' that Brazos Devil varmint, Marshal?" asked the old mountain man.

Nearby, Lord Beechmuir was emerging from the tent gripping a British Army pistol. The Sikh, Absalom Singh, was on his feet as well, holding that short, curved sword of his as if he was ready to chop up anything that represented a threat. Helene didn't come out of the tent, but Longarm wasn't worried about her. He knew she wouldn't be able to tell him anything he didn't already know.

"We got trouble," Longarm repeated. "Randall's dead. Somebody cut his throat."

"The hell you say!" Thorp burst out. "Where is he?"

"Back yonder in the woods a ways. I didn't strike a match to look at him, but I'd guess it happened pretty recent-like. Anybody hear anything unusual in the past few minutes?"

"Only you waking us up," grunted Thorp.

Booth shook his head. "I'm afraid I'm quite a sound sleeper, Marshal. Practically have to set off some dynamite to disturb my slumber, eh?" He looked at the Sikh. "Singh, what about you or Ghote?"

"I heard nothing," Singh replied, "and I sleep lightly, your lordship."

Ghote said, "The marshal has already questioned me. I know nothing about this matter."

"I sleep about like his lordship over there," Catamount Jack put in. "'Less'n there's some trouble, a bobcat could screech in my ear 'thout wakin' me up. How 'bout you, Lucy?"

"I didn't hear anything," Lucy said.

"Well, that's everybody heard from except Lady Beechmuir," Longarm said.

"Surely you don't think my wife had anything to do with killing that poor man!" said Booth.

Longarm shook his head. "Nope, I don't. That's what I was about to say. So what we got on our hands is a killer who

139

goes about his work mighty quiet-like.'' He bent over and lifted one of the branches from the fire. ''We'd better take a look at Randall, but I don't reckon there'll be anything we can do for him.''

Longarm was right about that. By the light of the makeshift torch, he and Thorp and Catamount Jack went to check on the body, leaving Lucy, Booth, and the two servants to watch the camp. Longarm was a little nervous about leaving Lucy around Ghote, since he wasn't convinced of the little Hindu's innocence—not by a long shot—but he didn't think Ghote would try anything now that the whole camp was awake.

Helene came out of the tent as Longarm and his two companions started into the woods. The lawman glanced back and noted that she looked disheveled but wide awake. He wondered if she'd gone back to sleep after her visit to his bedroll.

The corpse in the woods belonged to the cowboy called Randall, all right. Thorp cursed as the light from the torch revealed the man's bloodless face, which was frozen in a rictus of pain. Randall's throat was cut almost from ear to ear.

''Damn it, who'd do a thing like this?'' Thorp demanded.

''It wasn't the Brazos Devil,'' Longarm said. ''Not unless he's started acting mighty different than before.''

''No, I don't blame that monster for this.'' Thorp looked at Longarm. ''But that escaped prisoner of yours, that outlaw Rainey, might have done it.''

Longarm nodded. ''The same thought occurred to me.'' He didn't say anything about his suspicions of Ghote. He was going to keep those to himself for the time being.

Thorp heaved a sigh and shook his head. ''I don't reckon any of us will get much more sleep tonight,'' he said.

Longarm looked down at the body and nodded. He figured that was a safe bet.

Chapter 15

Morning couldn't come too soon for the members of the group. They were a sleepy-eyed bunch, Longarm saw as he knelt beside the fire and poured himself a cup of coffee. His own eyes felt gritty in their sockets, and there was a painful yoke of weariness across his shoulders. His head had started to throb again too under the bandage wrapped around it. He had to be careful about settling his Stetson on his head.

The Arbuckle's, brewed strong and black, helped considerably. Thorp was handling the cooking chores this morning, and he was frying up a mess of bacon and making johnny-cakes. He was a fair trail cook, Longarm judged, especially for somebody who had branched out into banking and gotten so successful that he sometimes wore town suits.

Catamount Jack and Lucy were both up and about, as were the two servants, but Lord and Lady Beechmuir had not yet emerged from their tent as the sun started peeking over the trees. Randall was there too, wrapped in a piece of canvas, his body a grim reminder of what had happened during the night. As soon as breakfast was over, they would bury him, then resume the search for the Brazos Devil. That seemed to be the only thing they could do.

"You going to keep on riding with us, Marshal?" Thorp asked as they ate.

Longarm nodded. "I've got to find Rainey," he said, "and sticking with you seems to be as good a way as any of covering the ground around here."

"Me an' my gal will partner up with you too," said Catamount Jack. "Leastways, if you're willin', and as long as it's understood we get that ree-ward if one of us brings down the critter."

"Of course," Thorp said with a nod. "My agreement with Lord Beechmuir made it clear that he gets the money only if he kills or captures the beast."

Longarm swallowed some food, chased it down with another swig of coffee, and said, "I've been thinking about that, Mr. Thorp. Seems to me you'd want to take the Brazos Devil alive. Otherwise how will you find out what happened to your wife?"

"That's true, Marshal," the rancher admitted. "But dealing with a monster like the Brazos Devil . . . well, it may not be possible to capture the creature." Thorp's tone was as bleak and cold as a frozen river as he added, "Besides, I'm enough of a realist to know how unlikely it is Emmaline is still alive."

Longarm was a little sorry he had pushed the man into that admission. For weeks, Thorp had been clinging to the belief—the hope—that his wife might be alive. Now, he was evidently coming to grips with the truth of what a far-fetched notion that really was.

Before the discussion could continue, the entrance flap of the tent was pushed back and Lord Beechmuir emerged. His distinguished, bearded face was set in angry lines as he stalked toward the others. Helene came hurrying out of the tent behind him. She caught up to him and reached for his arm, saying, "John, please don't."

Booth shrugged her off, ignoring her entreaty. As Lord Beechmuir came toward him, Longarm stood up. A blind man could have seen that something was wrong, and Longarm had a sinking feeling that he knew what the trouble might be.

142

He was going to try to be reasonable about this anyway. He said, "Mornin', your lordship. What's—"

Lord Beechmuir slapped him.

Longarm's head jerked to the side, as much in surprise as anything else. The slap wasn't much of a blow, but it was completely unexpected. Longarm's hands clenched into fists, and every instinct in his body cried out for him to plant a nice hard punch right in the middle of the pompous Englishman's face. With an effort that sent a tiny shudder through him, Longarm controlled that impulse.

"What the hell was that for?" he grated.

"I think you know quite well what it was for, sir," Booth said stiffly.

"Please, John," Helene said. "There's no need—"

Booth swung toward her for a moment, fixing her with a cold glare that made her fall silent. As his wife stepped back away from him, he turned toward Longarm again and said, "You have disgraced my honor, Marshal Long, and I demand satisfaction."

Longarm glanced at Lady Beechmuir, wondering how Booth could have found out what happened the night before if he had truly been sleeping as soundly as he'd claimed. Someone must have told him about his wife's visit to Longarm's bedroll, and the most likely person to have done that . . . was Helene herself.

Just for an instant Longarm saw maliciousness flashing in her eyes, and knew the truth. He had rejected her twice, and this was her way of getting back at him.

He looked at Booth again and said, "I swear I never did anything on purpose to offend you, Lord Beechmuir. I don't take kindly to being slapped neither, so I'll thank you not to do it again."

"I don't give a damn what you take kindly to, Marshal," Booth said with scathing sarcasm. "You made improper advances toward my wife, and I demand satisfaction."

That was the second time he'd said that, Longarm thought, but this just wasn't the time or place for such foolishness.

Besides, from what Booth had said, Helene hadn't told him the whole truth. To a stiff-necked Englishman, "improper advances" could be something as minor as a little innocent flirting. Longarm didn't think it was likely Helene had told her husband about crawling into his bedroll and giving him a fancy French lesson. She hadn't had to go that far to get Booth all worked up.

"What's this all about?" Thorp asked angrily. "We came out here to find the Brazos Devil, damn it, not to squabble among ourselves."

Lucy Vermilion was giving Longarm a hard look too, and he didn't want her getting riled up about this. He said bluntly to Lord Beechmuir, "Look, nothing happened between your wife and me. You'd better just let this go right now while you still can."

"Nothing?" Helene gasped. "Why, Custis, you call the things you said to me nothing?"

Lucy sauntered closer to Longarm. "Just what did you say to her ladyship, Marshal?" she asked.

Longarm grimaced, but otherwise ignored Lucy's question. This was a hell of a way to start a morning after a bad night. He was plumb out of patience. He started to turn away from Lord Beechmuir, saying, "If you don't want me riding with you anymore, that's just fine by me."

"By God, sir!" Booth burst out. "How dare you turn your back on me!" He grabbed Longarm's shoulder and spun the lawman around. "I demand satisfaction!" Once again, his open hand cracked across Longarm's face in a sharp slap.

That was more than Longarm could take. He didn't waste any more time thinking about it. He just sank his left fist in the middle of Lord Beechmuir's noble belly, then shot a hard right cross to the man's jaw when he bent over in pain. Helene let out a cry of dismay—or maybe deep down it was satisfaction—as her husband went stumbling backward from the blow.

Longarm didn't have a chance to appreciate the effect of the one-two combination. Before he even had time to draw a breath, something slammed into him from the side and he went down. He crashed against the ground near the fire, close enough to feel the heat from the flames on his face. Then he felt something as cold as the fire was hot, and it was pressing against the soft flesh of his throat. He looked up to see the bearded face of the Sikh glowering down fiercely at him. Singh had the point of that short, curved sword prodding Longarm's throat as he knelt beside the lawman.

The unmistakable metallic click of a gun being cocked sounded. Lucy Vermilion's voice cracked tautly across the clearing. "Better tell that fella who works for you to put away his pigsticker, Lord Beechmuir, or this Sharps'll blow his head right off in about two seconds."

For a nerve-wracking beat of time, John Booth said nothing. Then, grudgingly, he ordered, "Put the sword away, Singh, and let Marshal Long up."

Singh's lips drew back from his teeth. "If you ever touch my master again," he grated at Longarm, "I will gut you like a pig." He took the razor-sharp blade away from Longarm's neck, leaving a faint red mark behind where it had pricked the skin.

Longarm sat up as Singh straightened and backed off. He put his fingers to his neck, looked at the spot of blood on one of his fingertips, then said to the Sikh, "And if you ever pull a knife on me again, old son, you better use it in a hurry, because otherwise I'll gun you without even worrying about it."

"For God's sake," Thorp said hotly, "this isn't getting us anywhere."

"And we won't be going anywhere until my honor has been satisfied," Lord Beechmuir declared. He was standing and glaring at Longarm as he lightly rubbed his jaw. A bruise and a little swelling had already popped up from the punch Longarm had landed there.

Lucy eased down the hammer of her Sharps and lowered the powerful buffalo gun. She held out a hand to Longarm, who after a second's hesitation took it and let her help him to his feet. "Thanks," he grunted. "And not just for helping me up."

She nodded. They both knew what he meant.

"I thought you were an honorable man, Marshal Long," Booth went on. "What are you going to do about this?"

Longarm heaved a tired, disgusted sigh. "Just what the hell is it you want?"

Booth's eyes narrowed, and he said, "There's only one way to settle something like this. A duel."

Helene said, "John, no!"

Longarm chuckled humorlessly. "I thought it was just Frenchmen and Prussians who get so worked up that they have to fight duels."

"I know that we English have a reputation for being rather cold," Booth snapped, "but I assure you that our blood can burn as hotly as that of any other nationality. I've challenged you, Long, so the choice of weapons is yours. I should warn you, however, that I'm a crack shot with a pistol and was also the fencing champion at Eton for three consecutive years."

Longarm didn't bother pointing out that he had swapped lead with some pretty fair shootists himself, in situations where the only competition was to see who would live and who would die. He said, "I don't want to fight a duel with you, Booth, but I reckon if that's the only thing that'll suit you, I don't have much choice."

Lord Beechmuir's chin lifted. "You admit that you acted improperly toward my wife then?"

"I don't admit anything except that you're a bullheaded jackass . . . your lordship." It was Longarm's turn to let his voice drip with sarcasm.

"This is insane!" exclaimed Thorp. "We have to get on the trail of the Brazos Devil again."

Longarm turned to Thorp and assured him, "This won't take long."

"I should say not," Booth put in. "Well, Marshal, what about it? Name your weapon. Pistols? Sabers?"

"Neither," Longarm said, holding up his clenched fists.

146

"You look like you're in pretty fair shape. I pick bare knuckles."

The Sikh practically snarled and took a half-step forward, but Booth put out a hand to restrain him. "No, that's perfectly all right, Singh," he said. "The marshal is a few years younger than me, but I'm still perfectly capable of giving him a sound thrashing."

"We'll see about that," Longarm said curtly.

Thorp threw his hands in the air, shook his head, and turned away muttering disgustedly. Catamount Jack came over to Longarm and clapped a hand on his back, almost staggering the younger man. "Don't see as you had much choice, son. Try not to whup that Englisher too bad."

Longarm hoped he could just defeat Lord Beechmuir and get it over with quickly. He wasn't so sure, though, when he saw Booth taking off his shirt. The English nobleman's arms and torso were surprisingly muscular. Booth was older, as he had said, but it looked like he could give a good account of himself in a scuffle. Longarm left his own shirt on but took off his gunbelt, handing it to Catamount Jack.

"Aren't we even going to bury poor Randall first?" Thorp asked scornfully. "Not that I want to delay your duel or anything . . ."

Longarm looked at Lord Beechmuir. "The burying won't take long. All right with you if we wait?"

Booth nodded. "Of course. I can thrash you just as well half an hour from now."

Longarm let that one pass. He got a shovel from one of the packs, as did Thorp. They found a good spot on a hillside not far away. Catamount Jack followed and took the shovel from Longarm. "I'll handle this, son," he said. "You just save your strength for the tussle you got comin'."

It didn't take long for Thorp and the old mountain man to dig the grave. Booth left his shirt off, but draped one of the fancy buckskin jackets around his shoulders against the chill of an early autumn morning. Helene retreated to the tent and didn't watch as Thorp and Catamount Jack carefully lowered

147

Randall's canvas-wrapped corpse into the hole in the ground.

This burial, just like Benson's the day before, reminded Longarm too much of awakening when Rainey and Lloyd were shoveling dirt down on him. That seemed a lot longer in the past than just a few days ago, but the memory was still all too vivid for Longarm's taste. He never wanted to experience anything like that again.

Thorp said a few words over the grave; then he and Catamount Jack filled it up again. It wasn't much of a spot for a man to wind up, but according to Thorp, Randall hadn't had any family, so Longarm supposed this was as good a place as any.

"All right," Booth said impatiently when the burying was over, "let's get on with it." He strode down the hill toward the camp without looking back to see if the others were following him.

Lucy Vermilion fell in step beside Longarm. "You shouldn't be fightin' like this," she said in a quiet voice. "Your head just got kissed by a bullet yesterday. If that fella goes to poundin' on it, no tellin' what'll happen. You might get hurt real bad, Custis."

"Then I just won't let him hit me in the head," Longarm said with a smile. He sounded considerably more confident than he felt.

"You be careful," Lucy cautioned. "Don't let him get you down. I reckon a fella like that might try to stomp you."

Longarm figured Lucy might be right. He didn't intend to let that happen.

Singh had accompanied the others to Randall's burial site, but Ghote had stayed behind with Helene. The little Hindu was just emerging from the tent when the rest of the group reached the camp. Booth asked sharply, "Is my wife all right?"

"Her ladyship is distraught," Ghote replied, his voice as smooth as ever. "She does not wish to witness this combat."

"Well, that's her choice, I suppose." Booth's tone was gruff. "Still and all, it's her honor I'm fightin' for. I'll just pop in and see her for a moment.''

Ghote looked as if he didn't think that was a very good idea, but he folded his arms and moved out of Lord Beechmuir's way. Booth was in the tent for only a minute, and when he came back out his face was mottled with anger. "She's passed out," he said. "You've been giving her that bloody medicine again, haven't you, Ghote."

That accusation took Longarm somewhat by surprise. He had figured Lord Beechmuir knew nothing about his wife's fondness for whatever was in the bottle Ghote carried around. Evidently Beechmuir was aware of what was going on but didn't like it.

Ghote shrugged, unperturbed by his master's anger, and said quietly, "I serve her ladyship as well yourself, your lordship."

"Well, I'm tellin' you not to give her any more, do you hear me? Next thing you know, she'll be sneakin' off to some damned opium den like a bloody Chinaman."

The "medicine" was probably laudanum, Longarm decided. That was how many opium addictions got started. Helene wasn't going to be happy when she found out that her husband had forbidden Ghote to continue supplying her.

Of course, she was the one with all the money in the family. She could probably pay the servant to disregard Lord Beechmuir's orders.

Longarm suddenly wondered just who had given Helene the stuff in the first place and gotten her hooked on it. Having her so dependent on him for the laudanum would be a pretty lucrative arrangement for Ghote.

He put that question out of his mind. There were other things to deal with at the moment, like this damned fight with Booth. The Englishman turned toward him, stripped off the jacket, and asked haughtily, "Are you ready, Marshal?"

"If you're bound and determined to go through with this, I reckon I am," said Longarm.

"This clearing isn't really large enough," Booth said. "I propose that we go over to that field where there will be plenty of room.'' He pointed toward a large open area about two hundred yards downriver.

Longarm nodded. ''That's all right with me.'' He started toward the spot with Lord Beechmuir stalking along beside him. Catamount Jack, Lucy, an impatient Benjamin Thorp, and the two servants followed along behind.

Helene knew the feeling quite well. It was like swimming up from the bottom of a deep, dark pool. Mentally, she kicked against the forces trying to hold her down, pulling herself up toward the light.

At the same time, she didn't really want to go. She was content where she was, wrapped in the comforting darkness, unable to feel any of the pain and disappointment of life.

Reality would intrude its ugly face all too soon; why hurry the process?

Vaguely, though, she realized something was wrong. Some instinct was telling her that she had to wake up, that she had to leave the land of sweet nothingness behind and return to the harshness of the world. As she struggled to open her eyes, a bad smell filled her nostrils. Not just an unpleasant odor, she thought fuzzily, but an almost overpowering stench. . . .

She opened her eyes, blinked against the morning light that came through the open entrance flap of the tent. It had been closed when she lay down on the cot after drinking deeply of the medicine from Ghote's bottle. She was certain the servant had closed the flap behind him when he left. But now it was open.

Something moved between Helene and the light, something monstrous that blotted out the sun. Her eyes opened wider and her jaws spread apart in terror as she saw the huge, shaggy shape looming over her. A scream tried to make its way up her throat.

Then a filthy, hairy hand—or perhaps it was a paw—clamped down brutally over her mouth, cutting off the scream before any of it could escape. Helene tried to surge up off the cot, but it was hopeless. The strength of the thing holding her down was much too great for her to overcome.

This can't be happening, she thought, and just like that she had her answer. It wasn't happening. It was simply a dream brought on by the medicine, and soon it would pass. Even now she felt darkness creeping in around her again, blotting out the overpowering fear she had felt only seconds earlier.

She had known she didn't want to return to the real world, and she had been right all along. She slumped back now, welcoming the darkness, letting it wash over her and protect her, sealing her away from all the ugliness in the world.

Chapter 16

"This will be suitable," Lord Beechmuir said as he looked around the open pasture. "Plenty of room, eh?"

Longarm had fought a lot of battles in more cramped conditions, but he didn't mind the open space. As he took off his hat and handed it to Lucy, he made one final attempt to talk some sense into the Englishman. "We don't have to do this," he said to Booth.

"We most certainly do. Nothing else will satisfy my honor."

Longarm sighed and glanced at the others, as if to ask them what more he could have done to prevent this. Thorp just looked impatient, Lucy wore a worried expression on her face, and Catamount Jack was grinning with excitement and anticipation. Singh's bearded features were set in their seemingly perpetual scowl, and as usual, it was difficult if not impossible to read the expression on Ghote's face.

"Let's get on with it," Thorp snapped. "The sooner this is over, the sooner we can get back to looking for the Brazos Devil."

"Not to worry, Benjamin, old boy," Lord Beechmuir assured him. "I have a feeling we'll find that bloody beast today, and my hunter's instincts have never failed me."

Maybe not, Longarm thought, but Booth's inflated sense of pride was sure letting him down. The man ought to take a good look at his wife and see just what a fool she was making of him. But Longarm kept those thoughts to himself, knowing it was too late for them to do any good.

He flexed his hands and rolled his shoulders to loosen them up, then shook his arms a little. "I reckon I'm ready whenever you are, Booth," he said, no longer bothering to use the Englishman's title.

Booth lifted his fists and spread his legs in a boxing stance. "Have to, old man," he said.

"Up yours, old son," Longarm said, and threw the first punch.

It was a hard right cross that didn't have anything fancy about it, nor did it start from any Marquis of Queensbury position. It was the kind of punch Longarm would throw at some son of a bitch in a saloon brawl who was about to hit him with a whiskey bottle. His fist rocketed past Lord Beechmuir's belated attempt to block the punch and slammed into the Englishman's mouth. Booth went backward a couple of steps and sat down hard.

Singh's instincts made him reach for his sword again, but Catamount Jack casually let the barrel of the Sharps cradled in his arms swing toward the Sikh. "I wouldn't," the old mountain man said quietly. "This is between the two o' them."

His nostrils flaring with anger over his sweeping mustache, Singh took his hand away from the hilt of the curved sword.

Sitting on the ground, Lord Beechmuir shook his head, then reached up and gingerly felt his lips, which were bleeding and already starting to swell. "A good blow," he said in grudging admiration to Longarm.

"That's it, right?" Longarm asked. "First man knocked on his ass loses?"

"Oh, no," Booth said with a faint smile. "This battle is just beginning, my American friend."

"I ain't your—"

That was as far as Longarm got before Booth seemed to explode up off the ground and tackled him around the middle. Booth's shoulder rammed into Longarm's stomach, knocking the breath out of him. Both men went down hard, and Lord Beechmuir was already hooking punches to Longarm's midsection when they landed.

Longarm grabbed hold of Booth's shoulders and rolled to the side, throwing the Englishman off him. He scrambled onto his knees, then regained his feet just as Booth did the same thing. So far, Longarm had avoided being hit in the head, and he wanted to continue that. He pressed the attack, taking the fight to his opponent so that Booth wouldn't have time to plan any strategy. It was best to keep Booth on the defensive.

Unfortunately, Booth seemed to excel at that. He fended off more than half of Longarm's punches, and landed a jolting left-right combination of his own on the lawman's solar plexus. Longarm's injury had robbed him of some of his stamina, and he felt himself growing tired and winded. His arms were starting to feel like lead. Booth lunged at him, swinging a roundhouse punch at his head. Longarm avoided it just in time. The Englishman's fist whipped past Longarm's chin harmlessly, and for an instant Booth was off balance.

Longarm took advantage of that opportunity, grabbing Booth's arm, sticking a leg in front of him, and tossing Booth over his hip in a move taught to Longarm by his celestial friend Ki, who lived on Jessie Starbuck's vast Circle Star ranch in West Texas. Booth fell heavily on his back. Longarm landed in the middle of him with both knees before Booth had a chance to get up. He sledged a couple of looping overhand blows to Booth's face, rocking the aristocrat's head from side to side. Booth's nose was bleeding now, as well as his mouth. His eyes were glazed. Longarm sensed that the fight was just about over.

Somewhere, though, Lord Beechmuir found the strength to lift his right leg, bring it around in front of Longarm's neck, and toss the lawman to the side with a well-executed scissors move. Longarm's hands slapped the ground as he fell, catching himself before he could sprawl full-length. He scrambled around to face Booth again, pushing himself upright as he did so.

Booth was on his feet too, trying to lift his hands back into that formal boxer's pose. Obviously, though, he lacked the strength to do so. He swayed from side to side and said thickly through his swollen, bloody lips, "Come . . . come on . . . old boy . . . unless you're willing to . . . admit defeat . . ."

Longarm tasted the sourness of disgust in his mouth, disgust at Booth for provoking this fight and disgust at himself for going through with it. He spat, but that didn't help much with the taste. "I'm done," he said harshly. "I'm not giving up, but I'm not fighting anymore either. You take that any way you want."

"And you . . . you'll stay away . . . from my wife?" Booth insisted.

"You can damn sure count on that," Longarm said.

"And . . . apologize to her?"

"Whatever it takes."

"Smashing . . ."

With that, Booth fell onto his knees. He might have pitched forward on his face if Singh hadn't been beside him instantly, grasping his arm to support him.

"Did you see, Singh?" asked Booth. "I . . . I thrashed the bounder . . . just as I said . . . I would . . ."

"I saw, your lordship," Singh said gently. "You were magnificent, as always."

Catamount Jack came over to Longarm, who was flexing his hands again. The fingers would be stiff and sore for a while. The mountain man handed Longarm his gunbelt and said, "Purty good little fracas whilst it lasted. Not very long, though."

"Long enough for me," Longarm said bitterly. "I never should have agreed to any damn duel—"

He stopped in mid-sentence as he glanced past Catamount Jack toward the camp. Something was wrong there, but it took

155

him a minute to figure out what it was. Then the realization hit him.

The tent where Helene Booth had been resting in her drugged sleep had collapsed.

"What's happened over there?" Longarm asked, raising his hand and pointing at the camp.

Everyone turned to look. A puzzled frown appeared on Thorp's face. "Where's Lady Beechmuir?" he asked.

Longarm was wondering the same thing. The way the tent was flattened, he couldn't tell if there was anyone underneath the canvas or not. He saw some lumps there, but those could have been made by the cots.

"My God!" Booth exclaimed, realizing that something was wrong. "Singh, get over there right away!"

"Your lordship will be all right?" the Sikh asked.

"Yes, yes, just go!"

Singh broke into a run, pulling out his curved sword as he went. Randamar Ghote was right behind him, and the others followed closely. The only one who lagged behind was Lord Beechmuir, who was still unsteady on his feet. Longarm looked over his shoulder, saw the trouble the Englishman was having, and hung back. "Let me give you a hand," he offered to Booth.

For a moment, Booth glared at him; then the nobleman nodded abruptly and accepted Longarm's steadying hand under his arm. "I'm obliged, Long," he said stiffly.

They hurried along as best they could, and by the time they reached the campsite, Singh had pulled the tent aside to reveal that Helene was not there. "Dear Lord, what happened to her?" Booth asked anxiously as he and Longarm came up to the flattened canvas. Both cots had collapsed.

"Somebody tore down the tent while the rest of us were watching you and Long, your lordship," Thorp said. His voice rose excitedly. "Look!"

He pointed at some tracks on the ground. The marks made by Singh's boots had obscured some of the huge, misshapen footprints, but there were enough of them so that most were

156

still clearly visible. Longarm had seen them before, and the conclusion to which they led was obvious.

Helene Booth was gone, and the tracks of the Brazos Devil were all over the place.

Lord Beechmuir was almost insane with worry, not surprising considering what had happened. As the rest of the group made hurried preparations to break camp, Booth paced back and forth in a growing frenzy. The discovery of his wife's disappearance had made him forget all about the aches and pains he had received in the fight with Longarm. Thorp had offered him sympathy, since the rancher knew what he was going through, but the Englishman had seemed to barely notice.

"Never should have left her here like that," Booth muttered. "Should have gotten rid of that bloody Hindu a long time ago."

Longarm overheard the comment and couldn't disagree with it. He wondered how long Helene's addiction had been encouraged by Ghote. Her ladyship's dependence on him had no doubt given him quite a position of strength in the household. Longarm wondered too if the servant had been building up quite a stash of loot from what Helene paid him to supply her with her "medicine."

All that was a matter for Lord and Lady Beechmuir to work out between themselves . . . assuming they could catch up to the Brazos Devil and rescue Helene from him safe and sound.

While Longarm was saddling the Appaloosa, Catamount Jack sidled over to him and said in a low voice, "You know, Marshal, somethin' about them tracks we found strike me as mighty familiar."

Longarm looked quickly at the old mountain man. "You've seen something like them before?"

"Mebbe. I ain't sayin' for sure, mind you, but now that I've got a good look at 'em, I think maybe I have." Catamount Jack shook his grizzled head. "I sure can't recollect where or when, though."

"Maybe it'll come to you," Longarm said. He wasn't sure

157

what good it would do them if Catamount Jack had run into a similar creature before, but the knowledge might come in handy. It was hard to know what they were going to find.

Longarm estimated they were less than half an hour behind the Brazos Devil when they rode out of the camp. This was perhaps their best chance yet to catch up to the creature. The varmint must have been watching them, he thought as the riders trotted toward the river, following the tracks. Man, beast, or something in between, the Devil was obviously cunning and observant enough to have known that Helene was alone in the tent while the attention of everyone else in the party was occupied elsewhere.

The tracks led to the bluff overlooking the river—straight to the edge, in fact. Booth reined in and said hollowly, "My God, did . . . did the beast jump off the brink with Helene?"

Carefully, Longarm walked the Appaloosa closer to the edge and peered down, wondering if he would see the broken bodies of Helene Booth and the Brazos Devil at the bottom, killed in some sort of bizarre suicide. There was nothing down there as far as he could see, however, except a narrow strip of riverbank clogged with brush.

"Look there," Catamount Jack said, pointing. "You can see some sign where he climbed down."

Longarm studied the scratch marks indicated by the mountain man. The bluff was basically just an outthrust limestone ledge, and the face of it was quite rough. A man might be able to climb down it if he was careful.

But climbing down while carrying an unconscious Helene Booth was another story entirely, Longarm thought. That would take an incredible amount of strength and surefootedness . . . two qualities the Brazos Devil evidently possessed in abundance. The long scratches on the limestone looked like claw marks where the creature had searched for footholds.

"Is there a way down there?" asked Lord Beechmuir as he anxiously studied the markings.

"We'll have to ride north along this bluff for about a mile," Thorp replied, "but then we'll be able to get down to the river

158

again and double back. That's the closest way. Come on.''

The rancher put his horse into a ground-eating lope, and the others followed suit. Longarm found himself riding beside Lucy as the group strung out a little.

"I ain't overly fond of Lady Beechmuir," she said quietly to Longarm, "but I hope that critter don't hurt her much before we catch up to 'em."

"Maybe we'll be lucky this time," Longarm said. "The Brazos Devil obviously doesn't kill women right away when he comes across them, the way he does with men."

"Like I said before, maybe he's lookin' for a mate. Maybe Mr. Thorp's wife is still alive after all and the monster'll take Lady Beechmuir back to where he's got Mrs. Thorp hid out."

Longarm had a vision of a group of concubines, like some Middle Eastern harem, only presided over by some hairy half-man, half-monster instead of an Arab sheik. That was pretty far-fetched . . . but who was to say what was possible and what was not. He had run across plenty of things in his life he would have considered highly unlikely.

"I reckon we'll see, with any luck," he said to Lucy. "We ought to be at the end of this bluff pretty soon."

Sure enough, the ground soon sloped down toward the level of the river, and within a few minutes the searchers were able to slide their mounts down a short incline and then ride south again, this time following the narrow strip of riverbank.

The going was slow, however, because of the thick brush. It took more than half an hour to reach the spot where the Brazos Devil had climbed over the edge of the bluff with Helene. The only reason they knew they were at the right place was because Catamount Jack had tied a red bandanna on an upthrust finger of rock at the edge before they started riding along the bluff. The bright red cloth was clearly visible above them.

"Look for any tracks or signs that the beast broke through this brush," Thorp ordered. "We ought to be able to tell which way he went."

Several minutes of searching did not turn up any of the huge footprints, however. Nor was there a path broken through the bushes.

"Damn!" Lord Beechmuir exclaimed in worry and frustration. "The bloody beast can't have disappeared into thin air!"

Longarm frowned in thought for a second, then waved a hand at the rugged face of the bluff. "Maybe he worked his way along the ledge and came down off of it somewhere else."

Catamount Jack nodded and said, "That's the onliest explanation that makes much sense. If the critter come straight down here, we'd've been able to tell it."

"So what do we do now?" snapped Booth.

"I don't see any alternative but to split up again," Thorp suggested. "All we can do is ride up and down this bluff in both directions and look for some sign of the creature."

"Yes, but in the meantime, Helene is a prisoner of the beast!" Booth said hotly.

Thorp sighed. "Believe me, Lord Beechmuir, I know how you feel."

Booth took a deep breath, then nodded curtly and said, "You're right, of course. Sorry, old boy. I let my emotions carry me away. I won't allow that again." He lifted his reins. "Very well, shall we go? Singh, you come with me."

"We'd better string out along the river pretty good," Longarm said. "How long is this bluff, Thorp?"

"About two and a half miles, I reckon," the rancher replied. "From where we are now, it runs a mile to the north and a mile and a half to the south."

Longarm nodded. "I'll ride down to the southern end and start working my way back. The rest of you scatter out between here and there and each take a section of the ledge. We didn't see any tracks back to the north as we were coming along, so we'll leave checking it again for last, just in case we don't find anything south of here."

For a second, Thorp looked as if he was going to object to Longarm giving the orders. Then he nodded and said, "Sounds all right to me."

Longarm left the others to settle how they would split up the task of searching. He took the Appaloosa down the bank to the sandy streambed. He could make better time there than by sticking to the brushy bank, and he had the most ground to cover.

The river twisted and turned enough so that he was soon out of sight of the others, but he would be within hearing of a gunshot if any of them found anything. As usual, three evenly spaced shots would mean for everybody who could hear them to come a-runnin'.

Longarm wasn't sure how far the Brazos Devil could have come, working his way along the face of the rocky bluff, especially burdened as he had been by Helene Booth. But they had to cover every possibility. Longarm's own frustration was growing. What should have been a simple job had turned into a damned complicated mess.

But then life had a way of doing that, he reflected, and not just for deputy United States marshals.

As he rode along the river, he noticed another bluff rising on the western bank of the Brazos. It was almost a mirror image of the one to the east, he saw, only the limestone cliff to the west gradually became a bit taller. It was more rugged too, with shoulders and slabs of rock jutting out from its face.

Suddenly, Longarm reined in and frowned. It was not noon yet, but the sun was well up in the sky, its radiance washing over the bluff on the western side of the river. Longarm had spotted a patch of darkness on the face of that bluff, an irregular oval shadow that drew his attention for some reason. After a moment, he figured out what it was.

The dark patch was the mouth of a cave.

Longarm looked back in the direction he had come. The others were counting on him to search the riverbank on the east side of the Brazos, not to go gallivanting over to the west side. And yet, what better place to hide somebody or something around here than in a cave? Helene Booth wasn't the only missing woman, Longarm told himself. Emmaline Thorp was still unaccounted for, and had been so a lot longer

161

than Helene. Of course, even if the Brazos Devil had taken Emmaline to that cave, there was no guarantee she was still there. Or if she was, she might be nothing more than scattered bones by now.

Longarm grimaced and put that grisly thought out of his head. He would carry out his search of the eastern bank of the river first, he decided. He and the others could always return to that cave later and take a look in it. He started to swing the Appaloosa away.

That was when the late morning sun, shining so brilliantly on the opposite bluff, struck something shiny inside the cave and sent bright shards of light reflecting right at Longarm.

Chapter 17

He stiffened in the saddle as he stared at the reflection, then closed his eyes, shook his head, and looked again. Sure enough, the shiny brightness was still there. He hadn't imagined it.

There could be all sorts of explanations for what he was seeing, Longarm knew. A pack rat could live in that cave and could have dragged in some bit of metal it found somewhere: an old belt buckle, an empty tin can, damn near anything like that. The fact that there was something shiny inside the cave didn't have to mean a blessed thing.

But it would take him only a few minutes to find out whether or not the reflection was important, and Longarm had a very strong hunch he ought to do exactly that. One reason he had lived as long as he had, he was convinced, was because he knew when to listen to his instincts.

This was one of those times.

Longarm turned the Appaloosa toward the western bank of the Brazos and heeled the horse into a trot. He splashed through the shallow channel and across some more sandbars, then reached the shore. There was less brush here than on the other side, and barely enough room for the horse to stand after

Longarm dismounted and wrapped the reins around the trunk of a little mesquite tree. The steep slope of the bluff started climbing toward the Texas sky almost immediately.

For a moment, Longarm stood there and studied the face of the bluff, trying to pick out a good route that would lead him to the cave. He could still see the opening in the rock face above him, but not as well since he was almost directly underneath it now. When he had settled on his first series of footholds and handholds, he took a deep breath and started climbing.

The way was easier than he had expected it to be. Anybody who had grown up in West-by-God Virginia was part mountain goat anyway, Longarm thought. He ascended quickly, pausing every now and then to figure out which way to go next. As fast as he was climbing the bluff, there might as well have been a path hewn into it.

He was breathing a little heavier than normal from the exertion of the climb as he neared the cave. He stopped just below the entrance and inflated his lungs several times, replenishing his supply of air. Then he reached across his body and slipped the .44 from its holster. There was no telling what might be inside the cave, and Longarm knew from painful experience that a fella didn't go sticking his head into a dark hole without asking for trouble. He eased a little higher, to the point where he could almost see into the cave, then called, "Hello? Anybody in there?"

For a long moment, there was no response. Longarm was about to pull himself up into the entrance when he suddenly heard a low, muffled moan. His hand tightened on the grip of the revolver. He decided the sound was definitely human, not animal.

"I'm Deputy U.S. Marshal Custis Long," he called, not knowing if whoever was in there could understand him or not. "I'm armed, and I'm coming in there."

That was fair warning. He wouldn't feel any compunction about shooting back if anybody in the cave blazed away at him.

Moving quickly so that he wouldn't be silhouetted against the sky at the entrance any longer than necessary, he vaulted up and into the cave. As soon as he was inside he flattened himself against the wall on the right side, holding the pistol out in front of him, ready to fire. He had to stoop quite a bit, because the ceiling of the cave was only about five feet tall.

Longarm was aware that his heart was thudding rapidly in his chest and his pulse was pounding inside his head. His breath hissed between tightly clenched teeth. The cave was dim inside, but his eyes adjusted rapidly. He saw a small, shelf-like arrangement built on the other side of the cave. It served as a bunk for the shape huddled on it.

Long, lank blond hair told Longarm the person lying there was a woman. She was gaunt, her wrists looking painfully thin where they were lashed together in front of her with cord. Her ankles were tied as well, and there was a thick rope around her waist. The other end of the rope was fastened to an iron ring driven into the limestone wall of the cave, so that she couldn't move more than a few feet. The dress she wore was in tatters, revealing just how thin she really was. Longarm's eyes widened in horror at the idea of anybody being treated like this.

There was a black cloth tied over the woman's eyes, keeping her in perpetual darkness. She could hear him but not see him. He wondered if her mind was coherent enough for her to have understood him earlier when he called out his identity. Lowering the revolver a little, he said, "Ma'am? Ma'am, are you Mrs. Emmaline Thorp? Can you understand me?"

She gave that pathetic moan again and twisted her head on her stalk of a neck, trying to turn toward the sound of his voice. She writhed feebly on the bunk. Obviously, she was too weak to pull herself upright. Someone had been systematically starving her to death. As Longarm came closer to her, he saw faded bruises on her face and body as well. She had taken quite a beating sometime in the past.

"Mrs. Thorp, I'm a federal lawman," he said as he knelt beside her and holstered the gun. "I'm here to help you."

Most folks were skeptical, and often rightly so, when anybody from the government announced he was there to help. This time it was true, though. Longarm reached out and carefully, gently, worked the blindfold away from her eyes. She flinched violently from the light as it struck her eyes. Longarm knew it would take a moment for her to get used to it.

He glanced around the makeshift prison. On the shelf behind her was a glass bottle with a little water left in the bottom of it. That was probably what he had seen shining in the sun, he thought. The rays weren't reaching it now, since the sun had climbed a little higher in the sky. Only for a few moments each day would the light shine directly enough into the cave to reflect off the bottle. He had been in the right place at just the right time to see it. Only that stroke of luck had brought him here to this chamber of hellish captivity.

"You *are* Mrs. Thorp, aren't you?" Longarm prodded. He couldn't think of any other woman who might be held prisoner out here. She might be mad by now; if she wasn't, she was surely on the brink. He wanted to pull her back if he could.

Blinking rapidly, she managed to narrowly open her eyes. Her expression was more coherent than Longarm had expected. She was half-dead from her ordeal, so weak that she couldn't sit up, but she wasn't crazy. Her tongue came out and licked over cracked lips with zigzag patterns of dried blood on them.

"M-Marshal?" she husked.

"That's right, ma'am," Longarm said, relieved that she had understood who he was. "You're Mrs. Thorp?"

Her head moved a fraction of an inch, just enough for him to know that she was nodding.

Longarm grinned reassuringly at her. "There's been a lot of people looking for you these past few weeks, ma'am. Your husband's been mighty worried about you. I'll step outside and fire some shots to get the attention of him and the other folks with him; then we'll see about getting you loose from those ropes."

He drew away from her, intending to back out of the narrow

166

cave and signal the others. Helene Booth was still missing, but at least one object of the long search had been found. Emmaline Thorp stopped him, though, by reaching out and laying her hands on his arm. There was no strength in her grip; the fingers she pressed against his sleeve might have been nothing more than small bundles of twigs.

"No," she croaked. "Not . . . Ben . . ."

"But he can be here in just a little bit," Longarm said.

She shook her head, her motions more emphatic. She was drawing strength from desperation. "Not . . . Ben . . ." she repeated. "He . . . put . . . me . . . here . . ."

Longarm's eyes widened even more. He couldn't believe what he was hearing. He said, "But the Brazos Devil . . ."

"Not . . . Devil. *Ben!*"

Longarm looked around the cave again. The whole setup would have required some intelligence, all right. It was hard to imagine a creature such as the Brazos Devil seemed to be having the mental capacity to tie up and blindfold Emmaline like this, let alone leaving water for her so that she wouldn't die of thirst. The captivity had been designed to provide a lingering, painful, horrible death for Emmaline Thorp.

She was right. The Brazos Devil hadn't done this. Longarm knew that now.

But *Ben Thorp*? The woman's husband, the man who had raised such hell with Marshal Mal Burley in Cottonwood Springs, the man who had offered a twenty-thousand-dollar reward for the beast he'd said had stolen his wife?

What better way, Longarm thought grimly, to insure that Thorp himself wouldn't be a suspect in the disappearance of Emmaline and the murder of Matt Hardcastle?

"That son of a bitch," Longarm said under his breath. The whole thing had been some sort of perverted game. Thorp had put on a big show, when all along he knew right where his wife was. He had probably visited her from time to time, giving her just enough food to keep her alive so that he could continue to gloat over what he was doing to her.

Some men, Longarm reflected, were born to deserve a bullet

through the brain. Evidently, Benjamin Thorp was one of those men.

Longarm took a small clasp knife from the pocket of his jeans and started cutting the cords that bound Emmaline's wrists and ankles. "I'll sure get you out of here, ma'am," he told her as he worked, "and then I'll settle up with your husband."

"He's a . . . powerful man . . ." Emmaline whispered.

"Not powerful enough to get away with this," Longarm promised her. "You got my word on that."

When her hands and feet were free, Longarm tried to untie the knot in the thicker rope around her waist. It was too tight to come loose easily, however, so he started cutting through that rope too. As he sawed on it with the small blade, he asked, "Did your husband kill that Hardcastle fella?"

"Yes . . ." Emmaline's voice was as light and fragile as a feather. "He shot Matt . . . then used an ax . . . and a knife . . . to chop . . . to chop—" A shudder went through her at the memory, and she couldn't finish what she was saying.

"Damn," Longarm breathed. He hadn't seen Hardcastle's body, of course, but he had heard the descriptions of how the man had been torn apart. Evidently that had been some skilled butchery on Thorp's part, not only to conceal the bullet wound that had actually killed Hardcastle, but also to cast blame for the killing on the Brazos Devil.

That thought raised questions in Longarm's mind. Thorp might have been responsible for Hardcastle's murder and Emmaline's disappearance, but what about the Lavery boys? Who—or what—had killed them? *Something* had scared the hell out of Mitch Rainey that first day along the Brazos, and something had left all the various tracks Longarm had seen. Thorp wasn't responsible for the death of that gray gelding either; Longarm was sure of that. Nor had he carried off Lady Beechmuir—who was still among the missing, Longarm reminded himself.

Obviously, there had been more than one monster roaming along the banks of the Brazos lately.

Longarm's blade was nearly through the thick rope now. Once he had freed Emmaline, he could pick her up and carry her out of the cave. She was so light, it wouldn't be much trouble to make his way back down the bluff with her in his arms. Thorp must have picked this spot for her prison with ease of access in mind. He'd had to get her in here after killing Hardcastle, and if his plan had succeeded, eventually he would have had to dispose of her body.

"I'm sure sorry you had to go through all this, ma'am," Longarm said as he cut through the last strand of rope. "It sure beats me why anybody would do such a horrible thing."

The sound of a rock moving near the entrance of the cave warned him, but before he could do more than start to turn around in the cramped confines, something blocked the light and the metallic click of a gun being cocked echoed hollowly from the limestone. "I can tell you why, Long," Benjamin Thorp said. "I did it because the bitch deserved it."

Longarm turned his head enough to see Thorp standing there in the entrance. The rancher must have seen Longarm's horse tied up down below at the foot of the bluff, and had feared that the lawman would discover his wife's prison. So he had slipped up to the entrance of the cave, and now Longarm knew that unless he was able to turn the tables on Thorp, he might well wind up as another victim of "the Brazos Devil."

"Nobody deserves to be treated like this, Thorp," he said hotly, not so much to vent his justifiable anger as to get Thorp talking. As long as Thorp was gloating, Longarm still had a chance to save both himself and Emmaline.

"What do you know about it?" snapped Thorp. "I gave her a home, more money, nicer things than she ever would have had in that parlor house in New Orleans where I found her." It was hard to see the man's face with the light behind him like that, but Longarm could hear the sneer in his voice as Thorp went on. "Once a whore, always a whore, I guess. I'm not surprised she took up with Matt Hardcastle. But she could have had the decency to keep it from me! I might have been able to live with it if she hadn't admitted it to my face, hadn't told me that Matt was more of a man than I'd ever be!"

"It . . . was . . . true . . ." Emmaline gasped out.

"Shut up!" Thorp shouted. "Shut up, you slut! I don't want to hear your lies anymore. I listened to enough of them after I first brought you here to this cave. I listened to you swear that it was me you really loved, that Hardcastle didn't really mean anything to you, that you'd never betray me again. But by then I knew better, didn't I? I knew I could never trust you again. I knew all that was left was to punish you for what you did to me."

Emmaline started to sob, quietly, wrackingly.

Longarm's muscles ached from the awkward position in which he was frozen. He couldn't risk moving much, though, not with Thorp's gun cocked and aimed at him. If he had been alone in here, he might have taken a chance and thrown himself to the side, trusting that his own speed and accuracy with a gun would allow him to kill Thorp before Thorp could kill him. But in these close quarters, with Emmaline right beside him, he couldn't risk it. One of Thorp's bullets could easily hit her.

"What about the Brazos Devil?" Longarm asked. "What do you know about that, Thorp?"

"The same things you do," Thorp replied with a shrug. "There's something out here in these woods, but I don't really give a damn about it. All I knew when the Lavery boys got killed like that was that I'd found a perfect way to get rid of Hardcastle and punish Emmaline. I could do whatever I wanted, and everybody would blame it on the Brazos Devil as long as it was savage enough."

"And if we'd found the critter and killed it?"

"Then everyone would have believed that it dragged Emmaline off and killed her. Her body would never be found. That would end it all."

"That's what you wanted, wasn't it?" Longarm said. "That's the real reason for the bounty on the Brazos Devil

170

and for bringing in Lord Beechmuir. You *wanted* the varmint dead, so that all the loose ends would be tied up.''

Thorp laughed coldly. ''And it certainly made me look more like a loving husband who was worried out of his mind about his missing wife. I fooled all of you, Long, and I'll keep on fooling the others. You'll have to disappear, of course, but maybe everyone will think that the Brazos Devil got *you* too.'' He lifted the gun a little, the barrel looking as big around as the mouth of a cannon in the shadows of the cave.

Looked like he was going to have to take that chance after all, Longarm thought. Thorp was through talking. Longarm tensed his muscles, ready to spring away from the bunk as he grabbed for his gun.

Before either of the men could make a move, though, Emmaline surprised both of them. With a strength she shouldn't have possessed in her withered body, she exploded up off the bunk. Freed now, since Longarm had cut through the rope tied to the iron ring in the wall of the cave, Emmaline flung herself toward her husband. A hoarse scream ripped from the raw gash of her mouth.

''Mrs. Thorp! No!'' Longarm shouted as he threw himself forward, landing on his belly on the floor of the cave. His .44 was in his hand, even though he didn't remember pulling it from the cross-draw rig. He couldn't fire, however, because Emmaline was between him and Thorp.

The murderous rancher didn't have to worry about that. His gun crashed, sending bullets slamming into his wife's body at close range. The impact of the slugs should have thrown her back or at least dropped her in her tracks, but the rage and hate that had jerked her up from the bunk were too powerful to allow her to be stopped. Her arms outstretched, the claw-like hands reaching desperately for Thorp's neck, she ran full-tilt into him. With a startled yell, Thorp fell backward out of the entrance of the cave. Longarm scrambled to his feet and leaped out after them, the revolver held ready in his fist.

He didn't need it. Thorp and Emmaline were both tumbling head over heels down the face of the bluff, bouncing off rocks

171

but somehow staying together. A second later, they hit the ground at the base of the limestone cliff. The sound of the impact sent a wave of sickness through Longarm's belly.

He kept his gun out as he made his way back down the bluff, watching Thorp and Emmaline as he did so. Neither of them moved at all. When Longarm reached their side a few moments later, he wasn't surprised to find that Emmaline was dead. He had heard several of Thorp's bullets strike her. The midsection of her tattered dress was sodden with blood.

Thorp was dead too, his neck twisted at an unnatural angle. In falling down the steep slope, he must have hit his head and broken his neck. At least that was what Longarm sort of wanted to think.

Emmaline's fingers were still locked around her husband's throat in a death grip, and Longarm couldn't help but wonder if *she* had broken Thorp's neck with a burst of unholy strength.

Either way, Longarm thought as he slid his pistol back into its holster, they were both gone. This tragedy had played itself out to its inevitable conclusion.

But all the trouble wasn't over yet, and the sudden crackle of gunfire from upriver that made Longarm's head jerk up reminded him of that.

Chapter 18

The Appaloosa and Thorp's horse were both tied up nearby. Longarm ran to the Appaloosa, jerked the reins free from the little tree, and swung up quickly into the saddle. He wheeled the horse around and urged it into a run across the river. He didn't much like leaving the bodies of Thorp and Emmaline lying there by the river, but there wasn't much choice. He had to find out what the shooting was about.

He was afraid he had a pretty good idea already.

Being careful to watch out for patches of quicksand, Longarm got as much speed out of the Appaloosa as he could. He veered north before reaching the opposite bank. He could make better time by staying in the streambed, rather than trying to force his way through the thick brush along the bank. More shots rang out, and a few distant yells drifted to Longarm's ears.

Sounded like the others had caught up to the Brazos Devil at last, he thought.

The shooting stopped just as Longarm sent the Appaloosa around one of the bends in the river. He saw movement up ahead on the eastern bank and reined in sharply. He wanted to see what was going on before he charged in there. Edging his mount toward the shore, he leaned forward in the saddle and squinted as he peered along the river.

He saw the two servants standing near the edge of the bank; it was easy to identify them by their turbans. Not far away, in a clearing in front of what appeared to be another cave at the base of the bluff, stood Lord Beechmuir. He was facing Mitch Rainey, who stood near the mouth of the cave with a pistol in one hand and his other arm around the neck of Helene Booth. Rainey kept what appeared to be a tight, painful grip on her while he covered her husband with the gun in his other hand.

Rainey again, Longarm thought bitterly. He wished he had killed the outlaw a long time ago, when he had the chance.

Moving quietly, Longarm slipped down from the saddle and climbed onto the riverbank. He tied the Appaloosa's reins to a bush. As far as he could tell, Rainey hadn't noticed him yet, and Longarm wanted to keep it that way. If he could work his way through the brush along the bank, maybe he could take the fugitive by surprise and get Helene away from him before he hurt her.

Rainey's voice was loud enough for Longarm to make out most of the words as he began easing his way slowly through the thick growth. ". . . little lady tells me you're rich," Rainey was saying. "I want plenty of money and . . . head start . . . get her back safe and sound."

Longarm frowned as he continued moving closer. From the sound of it, Rainey had kidnapped Lady Beechmuir in order to hold her for ransom. But they had found the distinctive tracks of the Brazos Devil at the campsite after Helene disappeared, Longarm recalled. They had all assumed the monster had carried her off. But maybe the Brazos Devil had come along *after* Helene had been abducted.

Longarm gave a little shake of his head. They could sort it all out after Helene was safe and Mitch Rainey was dead, he decided.

"I don't have any cash with me," Booth was saying in reply to Rainey's demands. "At least not in the amounts you

174

suggest. I'm sorry, old man, but I can't help you."

"Well, then, I may just have to take this pretty little gal with me," Rainey shot back, clearly annoyed. "At least that way none of you bastards'll come after me. Speakin' of bastards, where's that marshal?"

"Marshal Long will be back shortly, and so will the rest of our party. You won't be able to get away, Mr. Rainey, so you might as well release my wife and make things easier on yourself when you're brought to justice."

Longarm heard Rainey laugh harshly. "Hell, nobody's goin' to catch me," he boasted. "Not as long as I got that new partner of mine."

New partner? Longarm thought. What in blazes was Rainey talking about?

A second later, Longarm's blood seemed to freeze as he heard Helene start screaming. He hurried forward, confident that her shrieks would now muffle any slight noise he might make moving through the brush. Just before he would have broken into the open, he dropped into a crouch behind the last screening bushes and parted the growth to peer through it.

Longarm's breath caught in his throat. Lurching out of the cave behind Rainey was something the likes of which Longarm had never seen before. The creature was stooped over, but if it had been standing upright, he judged it would have been close to seven feet tall. A thick coat of matted brown fur covered its body. Huge clawed feet left deep impressions on the ground as it walked. A low growl rumbled from the creature's throat as burning yellow eyes peered out of a forest of hair.

Was it a bear? Longarm asked himself. No, the bone structure was wrong, he decided. Some things about the monster looked almost human. Was it . . . could it be . . . a man? Longarm couldn't tell, but he understood now why Rainey had been so scared that other time and why Helene was screaming now. Just looking at the thing made cold chills prickle along Longarm's spine.

"My God!" exclaimed Booth. His face was pale and he

looked like he wanted to run, but he controlled his fear with a visible effort. "You're . . . you're in league with the Brazos Devil!"

"Yep, you could say that," Rainey replied as his grip on Helene's neck tightened and he choked off her screams. "Him and me got together yesterday. I figured he was goin' to kill me like he did those other folks, but he ain't so bad if you don't rile him. Him and me get along now, and he does just about anything I tell him to do, like grabbin' this gal of yours for me. He just don't like it when somebody tries to hurt him, or when they make a lot of noise. I reckon when those rancher's boys who got killed a while back happened on him, they tried to lasso him or shoot him or something like that."

"What about Marshal Long's horse?" asked Booth.

Rainey shrugged. "All critters got to eat. Out here in the woods, you take what you can get."

Helene was sobbing quietly now and shuddering in Rainey's brutal grasp. Longarm wondered if he could put a bullet in the outlaw's head from here, taking Rainey down with a quick kill. But even if he was able to do that, the Brazos Devil would still be right there to grab Helene. Longarm didn't think he could drop the creature with a handgun.

Where the hell were Catamount Jack and Lucy? A couple of Big Fifties would come in mighty handy right about now.

For that matter, Singh had his master's elephant gun slung on his back, but it would take time to bring the Markham & Halliday into firing position, time that none of them would have if trouble broke out. As far as Longarm could see, it was a standoff.

Then a slight motion caught his eye and he lifted his gaze to the bluff behind Rainey. Lucy Vermilion was up there, Longarm saw as his pulse quickened. She was working her way along the rugged face of the limestone, just as they had figured the Brazos Devil had done when it carried off Helene. Longarm didn't see any sign of Catamount Jack, but he figured the mountain man was around somewhere close by. Lucy must have come to investigate the shooting the same as Longarm had, and now she was trying to get behind Rainey without the outlaw seeing her. So far she seemed to have been successful. Rainey never even glanced in her direction.

Lucy had her Sharps strapped to her back. She reached a spot almost directly behind the group on the ground, and settled into a little crease where a boulder jutted out from the bluff. Longarm watched as she brought the Sharps around and lifted it to her shoulder, steadying both herself and the big buffalo gun. He wasn't sure what she intended to do, but it was obvious all hell was going to break loose around here in a matter of seconds. Longarm tensed and lifted his gun, ready to act as soon as Lucy made her move.

Unfortunately, Lord Beechmuir chose that moment to glance up, spot Lucy on the bluff, and exclaim, "Good Lord!"

Rainey twisted around, yanking Helene with him. The Brazos Devil turned too, just as Lucy fired. The Sharps boomed and the creature staggered, fur flying in the air from its left shoulder where the heavy slug merely grazed it. Longarm knew he couldn't wait any longer. He burst out of the brush and yelled, "Rainey!"

The outlaw didn't know which way to turn. He looked around frantically, uncertain which threat to react to first. Longarm couldn't fire with Helene so close to Rainey, but Booth lunged forward, grabbing for his wife. He shouted, "I'm coming, Helene!"

The Brazos Devil let out a roar and swung a thick arm with surprising speed. The backhanded blow slammed into Lord Beechmuir and knocked him sprawling. The creature bellowed again and lifted both hands, apparently ready to club them down on Booth's head and crush the Englishman's skull.

Before the blow could fall, Singh was there, slashing at the Devil with the curved sword. The Sikh shouted his defiance in as fierce a tone as the monster had. He cut and thrust with the blade as the Brazos Devil attacked, enveloping Singh in its long, heavily muscled arms.

In the meantime, Ghote was rushing toward Rainey and Helene. The little Hindu had a dagger in his hand, and despite

177

Longarm's dislike for Ghote, he had to admit the servant wasn't lacking in courage. Charging into the barrel of a gun armed only with a small knife was an act of bravery—or desperation. Maybe Ghote just didn't want to lose all the benefits he had gained from his mistress's laudanum addiction.

Rainey saw Ghote coming and triggered a quick shot at him. The bullet hit Ghote in the chest and spun him around. While he was falling, a groggy Lord Beechmuir regained his feet and threw himself at Rainey, crashing into the outlaw and loosening his grip on Helene. She jerked free and tried to run, making only a few feet before she stumbled and fell.

But that took her out of the line of fire, and Longarm yelled at her husband, "Get down, Booth!"

Lord Beechmuir didn't have much choice in the matter. Rainey slashed at him with the gun and the barrel raked along the side of Booth's head. The Englishman fell.

For the first time, Longarm had a wide-open shot as Rainey turned toward him again. He took it, triggering twice before the outlaw could fire. Both slugs thudded into Rainey's chest and drove him backward. His eyes widened in pain and shock, but he still tried to lift his pistol and bring it to bear on Longarm.

The next instant, Rainey's head practically exploded as Lucy Vermilion's Sharps blasted again. The slug bored through the outlaw's brain and burst out the other side of his skull. The gruesome corpse swayed there for a second, already dead but not aware of it yet, before it slowly toppled over.

The Brazos Devil was still bellowing as Singh hacked at it. The creature's arms had completely encircled the Sikh and were crushing him mercilessly. Blood welled from Singh's mouth and nose as his bones splintered and his organs were pulped. But his arms kept rising and falling with the curved blade, which was now dripping with gore.

Longarm saw Catamount Jack appear at the other side of the clearing, behind the Brazos Devil. The mountain man lifted his Sharps, sighted, and pulled the trigger. The bullet slammed into the monster's back and knocked it forward. Its arms lost their grip on Singh and he slid limply to the ground. Ponderously, the Brazos Devil swung around toward Catamount Jack, whose eyes widened in shock.

"Luther?" said Catamount Jack.

The Brazos Devil roared and stumbled toward the mountain man. Longarm emptied his .44 into the creature's side, staggering it but not knocking it down. The thick brown fur was covered with blood now from the bullet and sword wounds, but the Brazos Devil was still on its feet, still bent on mayhem. Longarm wondered if it *could* be killed.

But if it drew breath, cold steel could kill it. Longarm jammed his gun back in its holster and ran forward, bending over to snatch up the sword Singh had dropped. He wrapped both hands around its hilt and lifted it over his head as he lunged at the Brazos Devil. With a primitive yell of his own, he drove the blade into the back of the creature as hard as he could. This close, the stench of the beast was almost enough to overpower a man.

The Devil had just reached Catamount Jack, who had drawn a Bowie knife from a sheath at his waist. Catamount Jack plunged the Bowie into the creature's chest at the same time as Longarm attacked from behind. The Brazos Devil roared in pain and rage and flailed around with its arms. One of them clipped Longarm and knocked him backward, off his feet.

"Get back, Pa!" Lucy called, and a second later the Sharps boomed yet again. Longarm heard the thud as the slug struck the Brazos Devil, but he didn't know where the shot had landed on the creature. All he knew was that the monster was still on its feet, even with a Bowie knife sticking out of its chest and the Sikh's sword protruding from its back. It looked around at the circle of humans around it, then threw back its head and let out a pitiful howl that died away into a whimper. It stumbled a couple of steps, then went to its knees. The Brazos Devil gave a shake of its shaggy head.

Longarm got to his feet and watched along with Catamount Jack and Lucy as the creature fell slowly onto its side like a huge tree. Its breath rasped harshly in its throat for a few seconds, then stopped. A shudder went through the massive body, but after that it was utterly still.

"I reckon he's dead," Catamount Jack said into the hushed silence that followed. "Poor son of a bitch. Hope he's found peace at last."

Longarm looked at the old mountain man with a frown. "I heard you call it Luther. You knew that . . . that thing?"

"He's not a thing," Catamount Jack said solemnly. "He's a man. Leastways, he used to be. Him and me, we was friends a long time ago, back in the days when the buffalo still roamed the plains."

Longarm was still out of breath, and his pulse was hammering in his head. He started to reload his gun with cartridges from his shell belt, and looked around as he did so. Lord and Lady Beechmuir were standing nearby. Booth's arms were around Helene, and she was crying as she pressed her face against his chest. The Englishman was doing what he could to comfort her. He appeared to be all right.

Rainey was dead, of course, and so were Singh and Ghote. Longarm felt a touch of regret as he looked at the Sikh's crushed, misshapen body. Singh had been a hell of a fighting man, upholding the reputation of his kinsmen.

Longarm holstered his gun and turned back to the fallen Brazos Devil. Catamount Jack had hold of one of the man's feet. With a yank, he dislodged the clawed extremity. It was a boot of sorts, Longarm saw now, with what was evidently the paw of a bear attached to it.

"Them tracks we saw put me in mind of these special-made boots ol' Luther used to wear," said Catamount Jack. "I never thought it could be him, though. We used to hunt buffalo together, up in Kansas and the Texas Panhandle. I lost track of him 'bout six years ago, round the time the last of the big herds disappeared. He weren't right in the head even then, I reckon. Sometimes he claimed he *was* a buffalo. That's why he dressed in them skins."

"What was his name?" Longarm asked quietly.

"Luther Barcroft." Catamount Jack shook his head. "Ain't

180

no tellin' how he wound up down here in the Brazos country. Must've just drifted around after he lost his mind, gettin' farther and farther away from folks.'' With a sigh, Catamount Jack added, ''I ain't sure I'd feel right collectin' a bounty on an old friend like this, but I reckon you and me and Lucy got it comin', Marshal. And that feller over there who had the sword, if he's got any kin that can claim it.''

''We don't have to worry about that,'' Longarm said bleakly. ''There won't be any bounty. Nobody to pay it. Thorp's dead.''

''Dead?'' Lucy repeated in surprise as she came up to them. ''What happened to him?''

''I found his wife,'' Longarm said. ''She's dead too, though. It's a long story, and it's sure not pretty.''

Catamount Jack opened the breech of his Sharps and started reloading it. ''You mean to say ever'body's dead 'ceptin' us three and them two English folks?''

Longarm nodded. ''Looks like it.''

Catamount Jack shook his head. ''I reckon I've had enough of monsters and such.''

''So have I,'' Longarm said tiredly. ''So have I.''

''I'm still not sure I've got the straight of all of it,'' Marshal Mal Burley said late that afternoon. He and Longarm were in the little office in front of the jail in Cottonwood Springs, and Longarm had just explained everything that had happened. He didn't blame Burley for having trouble grasping all the bizarre turns this case had taken. Right from the start, when Longarm woke up facedown in that grave, the whole business had seemed like the kind of nightmare a fella would get after eating some bad beef.

Maybe that was it, Longarm thought with a faint, weary smile. Maybe the whole thing had been just a bad dream.

He knew it had been real, though. All too real . . .

''I'll have the fella who plays the typewriter in my boss's office send you a copy of the report I turn in when I get back to Denver,'' Longarm said. ''Old Henry won't mind—too

181

much—and then you'll have something official if there are ever any questions about any of it."

Burley nodded. "I'd be much obliged for that, Marshal." He shook his head. "Ben Thorp dead . . . that's hard to believe."

"Reckon you can go about your business now without worrying whether or not Thorp's going to like it." Longarm knew the comment was a bit rough, but he hated to see a lawman under the thumb of some rich, influential citizen.

For a second, Burley looked like he was going to take offense, but then he sighed and nodded. "Yeah," he said. "I reckon you're right. I hope I'm up to it."

"I've got a hunch you will be," Longarm said as he stood up.

He lit a cheroot as he left the office and turned toward the hotel. Earlier, he had left Lord and Lady Beechmuir there, and the doctor had been checking Helene to make sure she wasn't injured. Longarm was confident she was all right, other than being shaken up and scared half out of her wits. All the way back into town, she had clung to her husband and pleaded with him to take care of her, to never let her go.

If that attitude lasted, then something good might come out of the ordeal after all. Booth and Helene would need to be closer than they had ever been if they were both going to find the strength they would need to break Helene's addiction. Longarm wished them the best of luck, but he didn't particularly care if he ever saw either one of them again.

He regretted the deaths of everyone except Thorp and Rainey. He even regretted the death of Randamar Ghote, as unlikable as the oily little cuss had been. Some folks might say that Emmaline Thorp was better off dead, after what she had gone through, but Longarm couldn't bring himself to see it that way. Maybe . . . just maybe . . . some folks were so bad off that death was the best way out for them. Longarm had never been able to fully accept that idea, though. He drew on the cheroot, savoring the rich flavor of it, and thought about all the good things in life: the touch of a woman, the laughter

182

of a little kid, the air on a spring morning in the high country when the wildflowers were blooming. . . .

The way Longarm saw it, there was nearly always *something* to live for. And he intended to go on doing it for a long time to come.

He was still pondering the matter when he let himself into his hotel room a few minutes later. As he stepped into the room, he stopped in his tracks and looked at the big tin washtub in the center of the floor. It was filled with hot water, soapsuds, and Lucy Vermilion.

"How the hell'd you know?" Longarm blurted. "The clerk downstairs just rented me this room!"

Lucy smiled at him. "Who do you think slipped that slick-haired fella four bits just to make sure you got this room? I figured after everything we'd been through, you might want to clean up a mite."

A grin spread over Longarm's face. He threw back his head and laughed, then went forward to meet Lucy as she rose from the washtub, all pink skin and blond hair and feathery white soapsuds. He was naked by the time he got there.

Yep, he thought as he stepped into the hot water and drew her into his arms, there were definitely some good things worth living for.

And then he didn't waste any more time or energy philosophizing about it.

Watch for

LONGARM AND THE ANGEL OF INFERNO

208th in the bold LONGARM series
from Jove

Coming in April!

If you enjoyed this book, subscribe now and get...

TWO FREE

A $7.00 VALUE—

If you would like to read more of the very best, most exciting, adventurous, action-packed Westerns being published today, you'll want to subscribe to True Value's Western Home Subscription Service.

Each month the editors of True Value will select the 6 very best Westerns from America's leading publishers for special readers like you. You'll be able to preview these new titles as soon as they are published, *FREE* for ten days with no obligation!

TWO FREE BOOKS

When you subscribe, we'll send you your first month's shipment of the newest and best 6 Westerns for you to preview. With your first shipment, two of these books will be yours as our introductory gift to you absolutely *FREE* (a $7.00 value), regardless of what you decide to do. If

you like them, as much as we think you will, keep all six books but pay for just 4 at the low subscriber rate of just $2.75 each. If you decide to return them, keep 2 of the titles as our gift. No obligation.

Special Subscriber Savings

When you become a True Value subscriber you'll save money several ways. First, all regular monthly selections will be billed at the low subscriber price of just $2.75 each. That's at least a savings of $4.50 each month below the publishers price. Second, there is never any shipping, handling or other hidden charges—*Free home delivery*. What's more there is no minimum number of books you must buy, you may return any selection for full credit and you can cancel your subscription at any time. A TRUE VALUE!